Stage Dreams

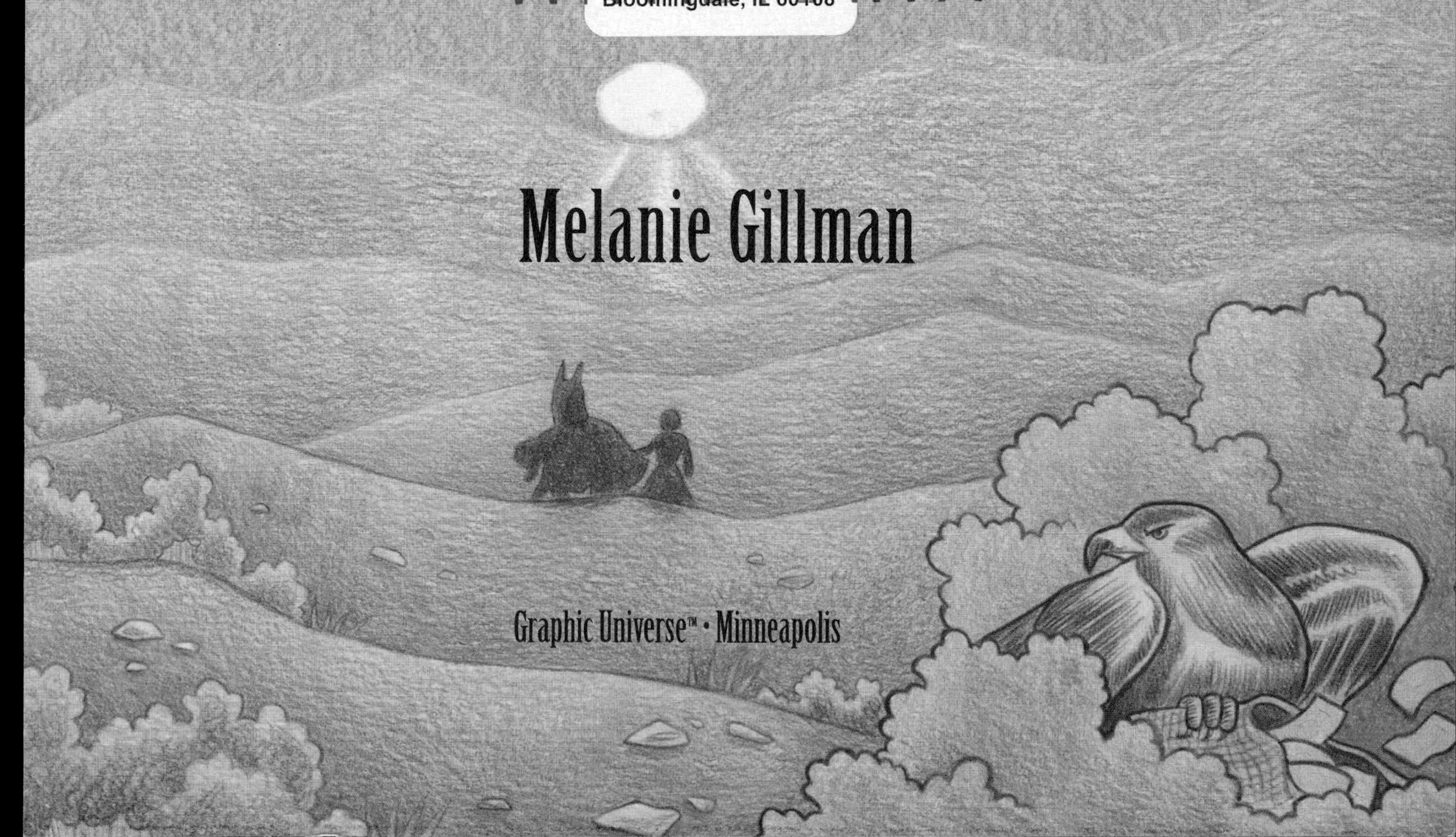

Melanie Gillman

Graphic Universe™ · Minneapolis

Graphic Universe™ is a trademark of Lerner Publishing Group, Inc.

Graphic Universe™
An imprint of Lerner Publishing Group, Inc.
241 First Avenue North
Minneapolis, MN 55401 USA

For reading levels and more information, look up this title at www.lernerbooks.com.

Image credit: The Granger Collection, New York, p. 92.

Library of Congress Cataloging-in-Publication Data

Names: Gillman, Melanie, author, illustrator.
Title: Stage dreams / Melanie Gillman.
Description: Minneapolis : Graphic Universe, [2019] | Summary: In 1861, Grace, a runaway,
    and Flor, a stagecoach robber, join forces to thwart a plan by the Confederate Army in
    the New Mexico Territory.
Identifiers: LCCN 2018052140 (print) | LCCN 2018056240 (ebook) | ISBN 9781541561113
    (eb pdf) | ISBN 9781512440003 (lb : alk. paper) | ISBN 9781541572843 (pb : alk. paper)
Subjects: LCSH: Graphic novels. | CYAC: Graphic novels. | Robbers and outlaws—
    Fiction. | Runaways—Fiction. | Transgender people—Fiction. | Confederate States of
    America—Army—Fiction. | New Mexico—History—1848—Fiction.
Classification: LCC PZ7.7.G543 (ebook) | LCC PZ7.7.G543 St 2019 (print) | DDC
    741.5/973—dc23

LC record available at https://lccn.loc.gov/2018052140

Manufactured in the United States of America
1-42258-26121-2/11/2019

To our queer and trans ancestors. Far too many
of your stories were lost, but we remember you.

MAP OF NEW MEXICO TERRITORY 1861

UTAH TERRITORY
COLORADO TERRITORY
CALIFORNIA
ARIZONA TERRITORY
WASATACH MTNS
VIRGIN RIVER
COLORADO RIVER
CHIQUITO RIVER
CANYON DE CHELLY
BASALTIC BUTTES
FORT DEFIANCE
SAN JUAN RIVER
RIO GRANDE
TAOS
SANGRE DE CRISTO MTNS
SANTA FE
FORT UNION
ALBUQUERQUE
FORT CRAIG
CANADIAN RIVER
BILL WILLIAMS RIVER
RIO SAN FRANCISCO
MOGOLLON MOUNTAINS
ZUNI MTNS
FORT CONRAD
RIO PECOS
GENERAL SIBLEY'S CONFEDERATE INVASION ROUTE

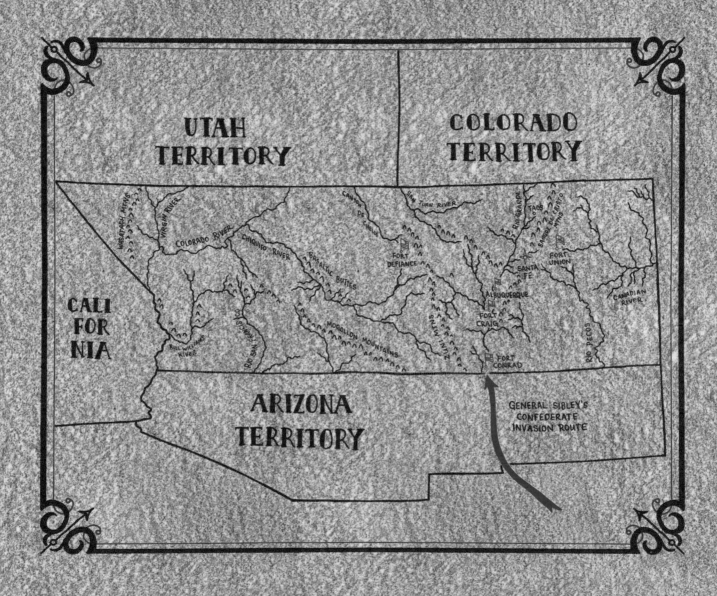

CHAPTER ONE

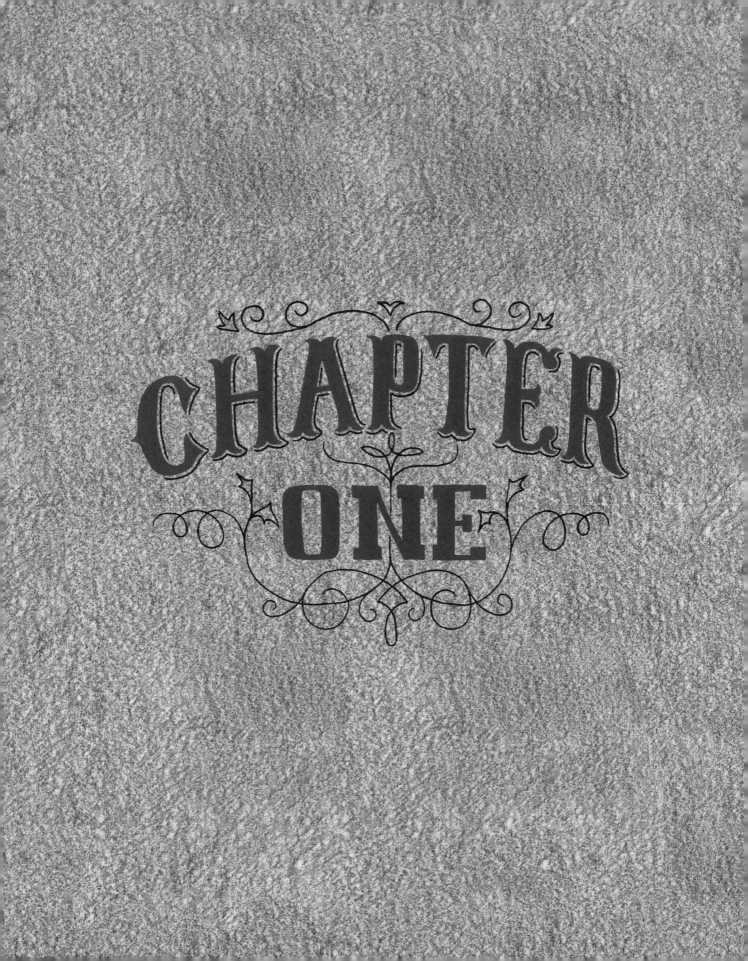

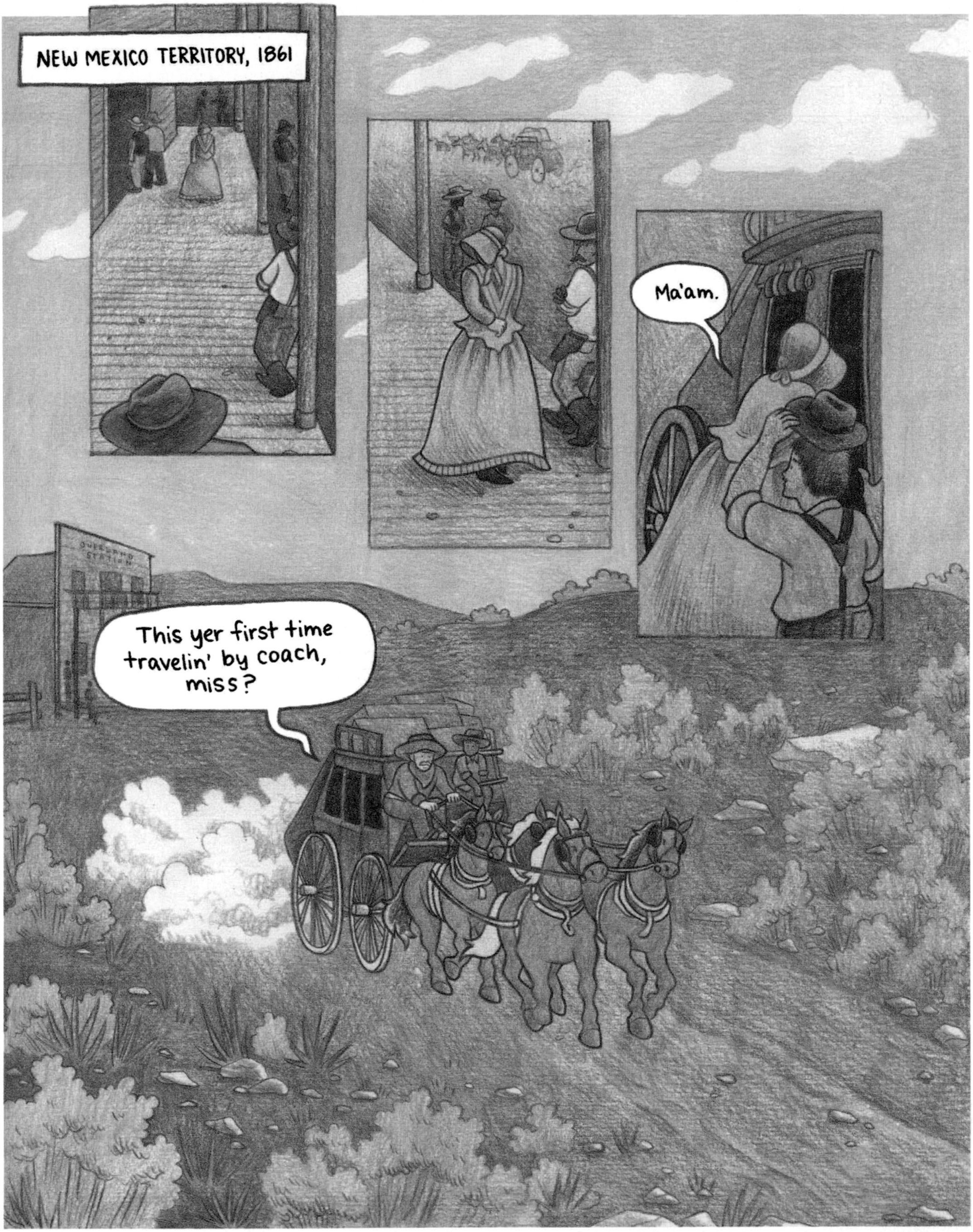
NEW MEXICO TERRITORY, 1861
Ma'am.
This yer first time travelin' by coach, miss?

I'm going to Arizona, to enlist under General Sibley!

pft

There's the Confederacy's grand plan for ya, then. Takin' over all New Mexico Territory with an army of *whelps*.

I'm s— eighteen!!

Pounds, maybe.

Leave the boy be.

It's a noble thing at any age— fighting for the liberation of one's homeland.

Sorry— liberation for *who*, again?

Everyone knows General Sibley'll only need a couple weeks to take New Mexico Territory, tops!!

Those Yanks in Arizona rolled over without a fight as soon as his Texans showed up—

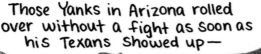

Siddown, boy—

An' now he's seized all the guns 'n' artillery from the Union forts, it's gonna be over lickety-split!

'Cept for the Apach' givin' him hell fror here to El Paso—

GONNA B ANY DAY NOW!

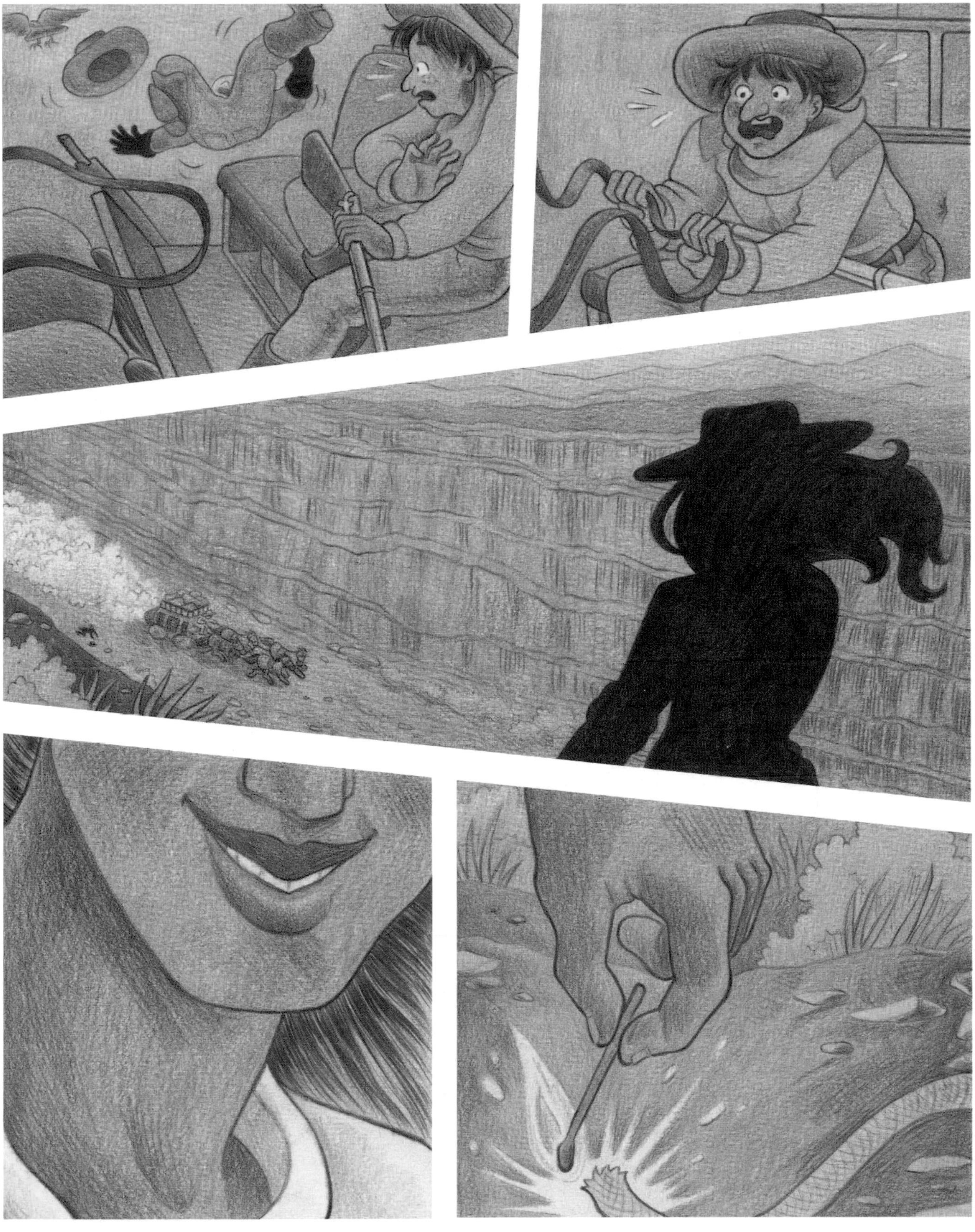

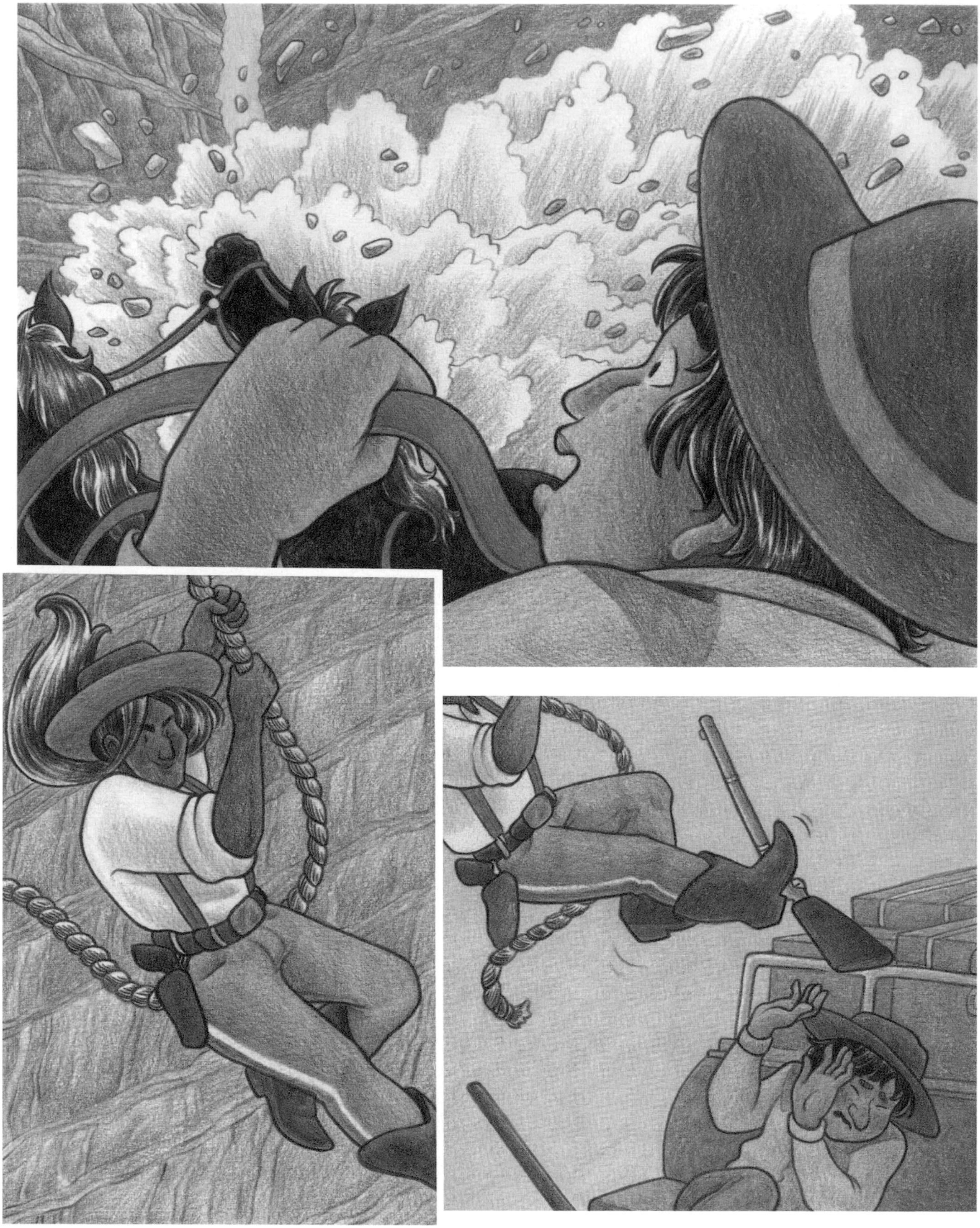

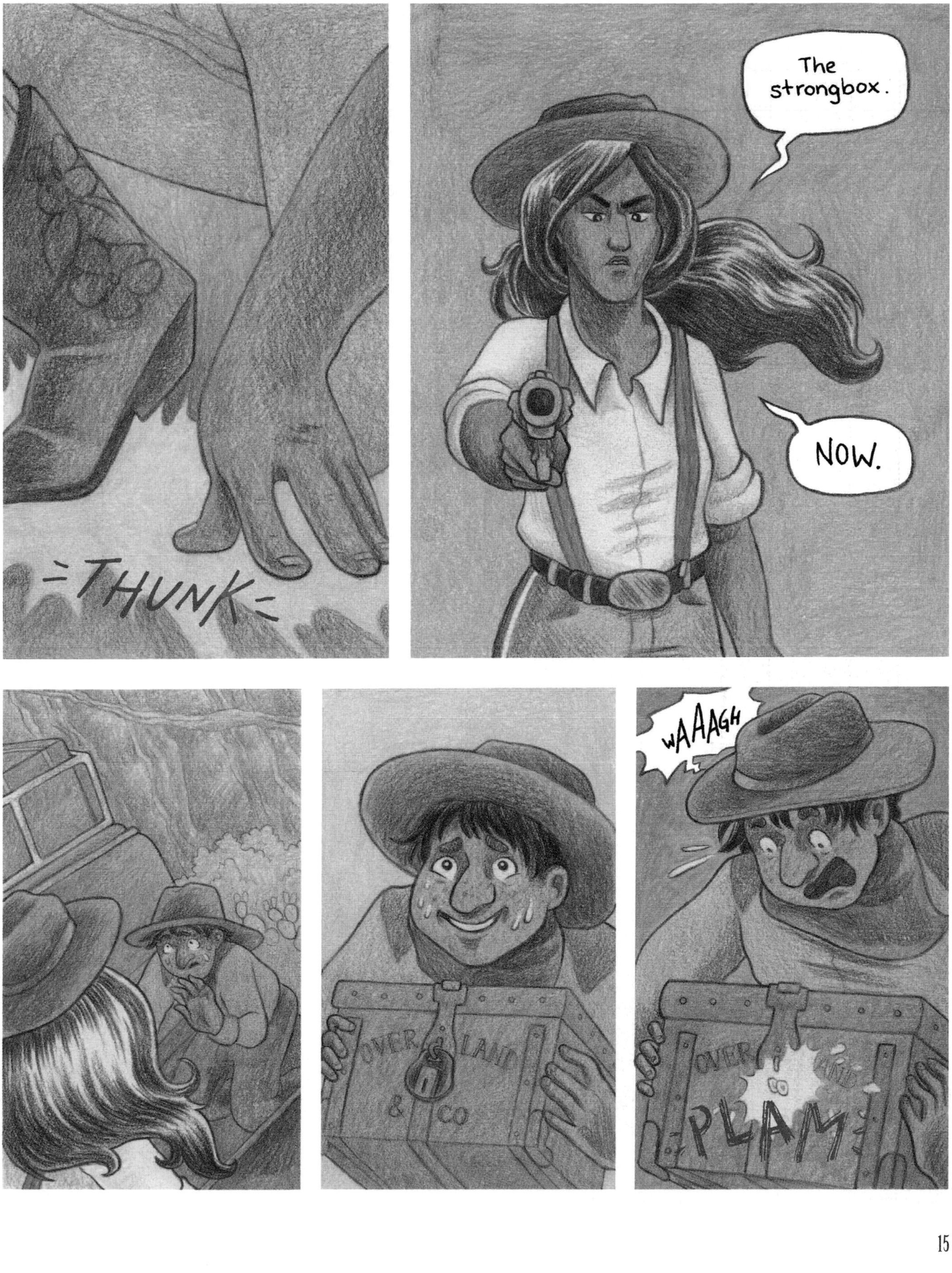
THUNK
The strongbox.
NOW.
OVER LAND & CO
wAAAGH
OVER LAND CO
PLAM

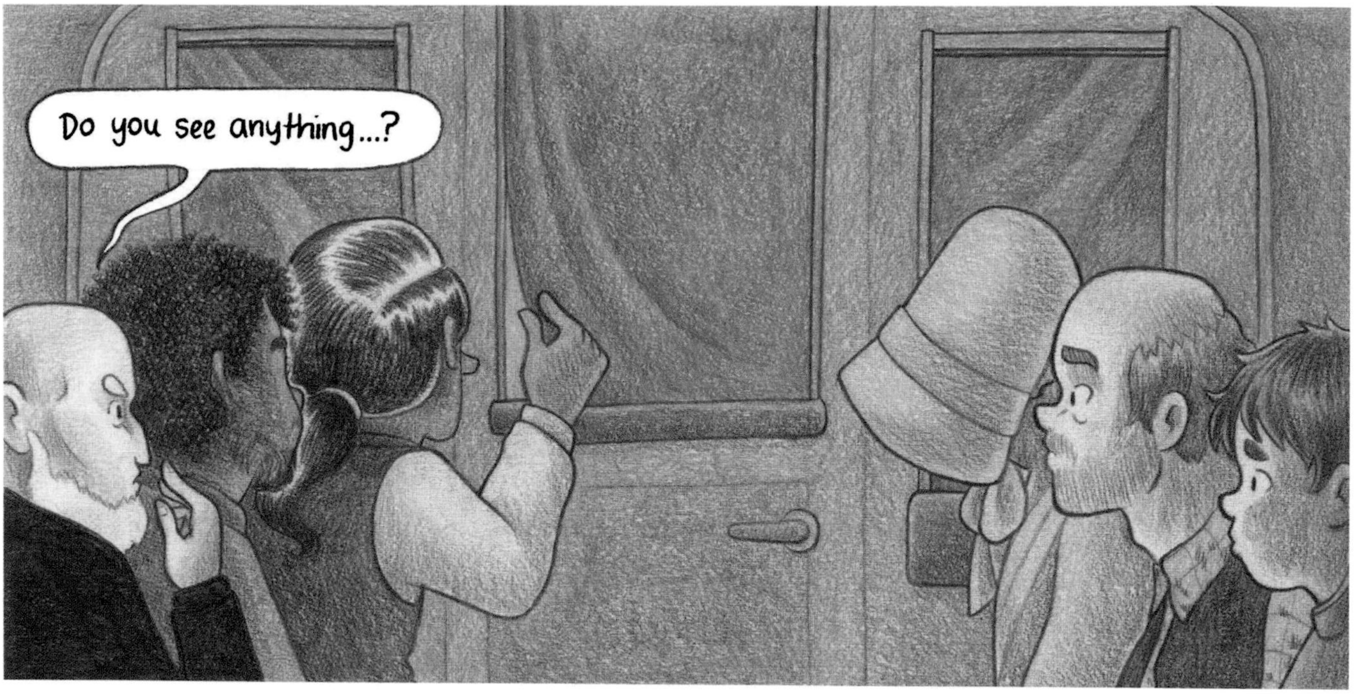
Do you see anything...?

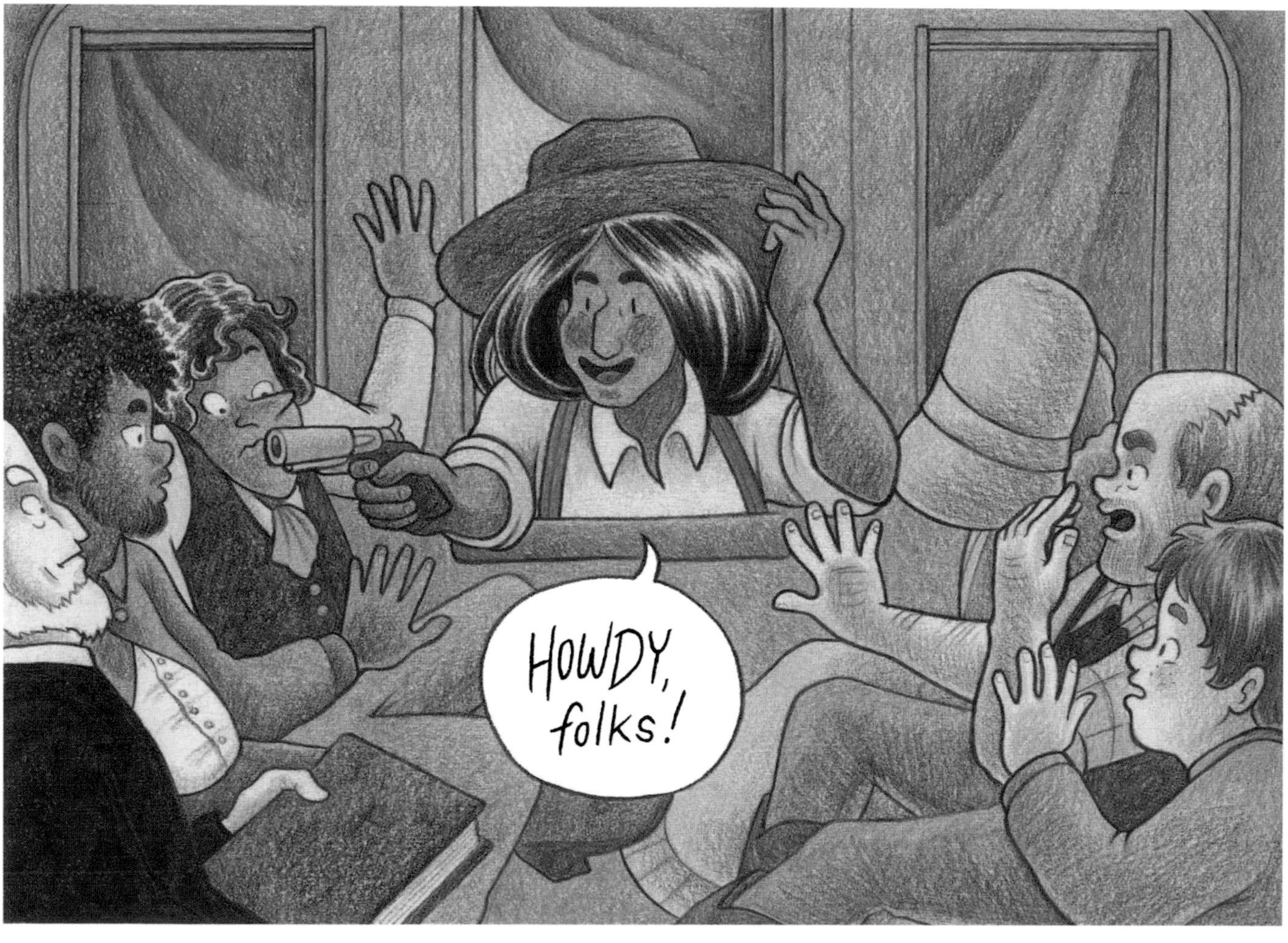
HOWDY, folks!

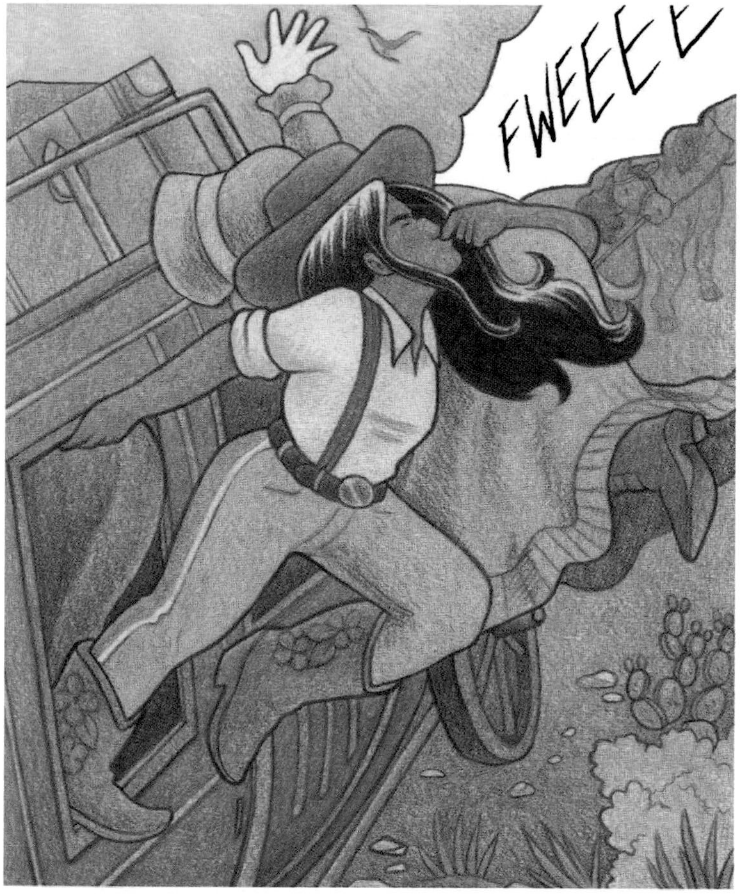
FWEEEE

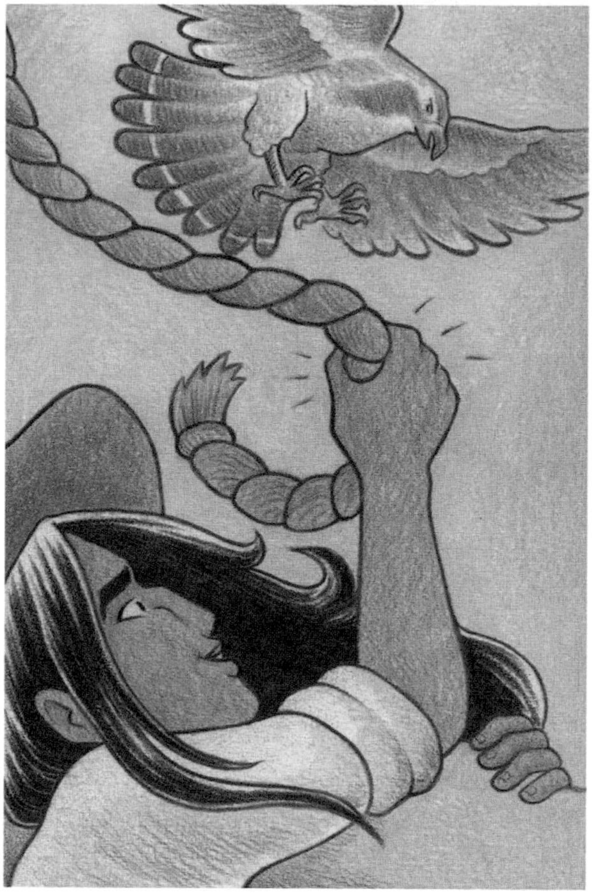

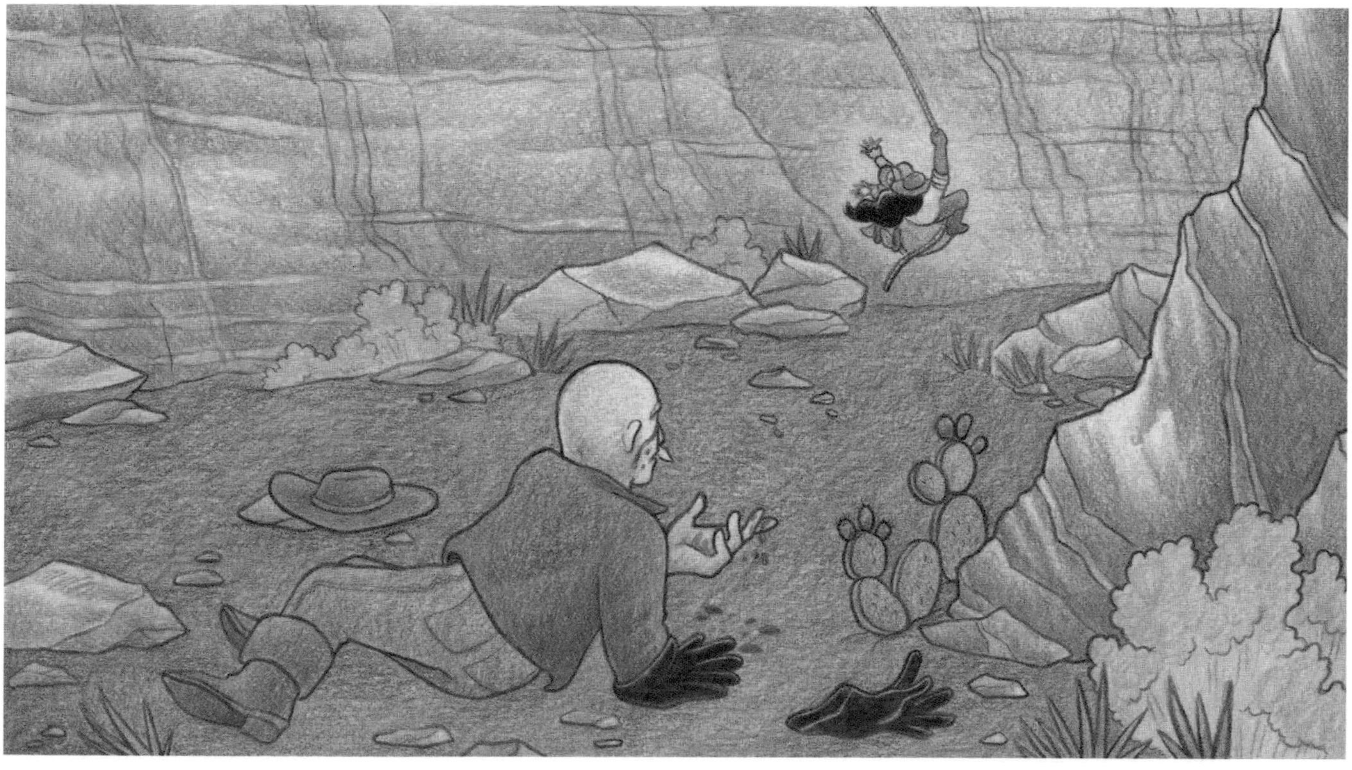

CHAPTER TWO

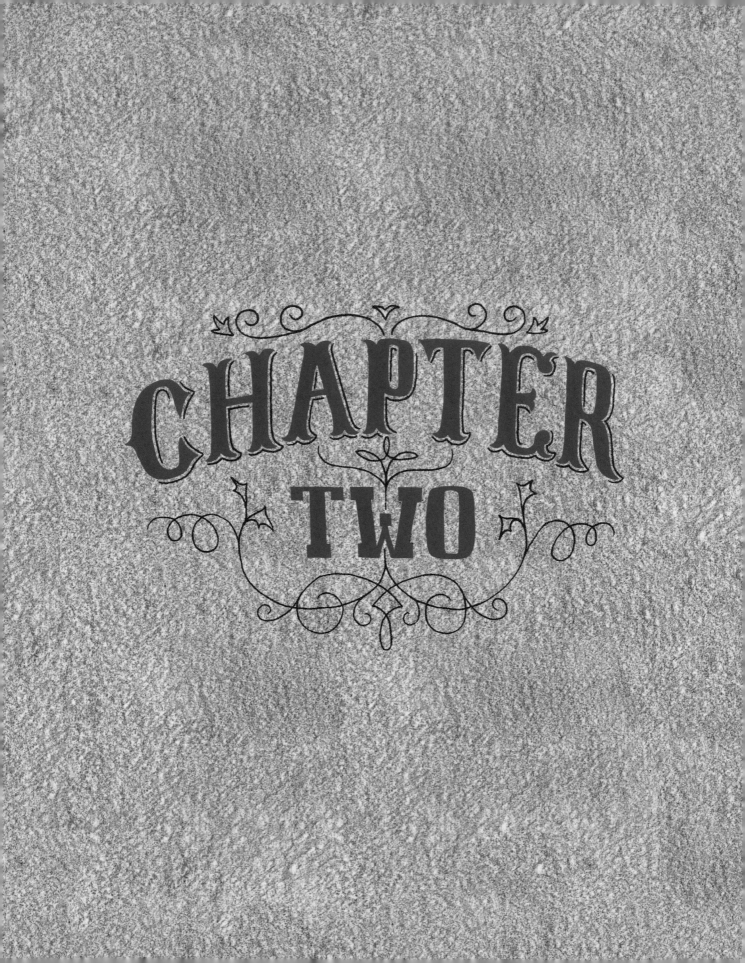

Those poor boys up at Fort Union have been *very* nervous since the Rebs took Arizona.

So I figured they might be *keenly* interested to hear what a bunch of Southern rail barons talk about when they think no one's listening.

But I can't risk a Confederate runaway telling anyone about the plan—

—So if I can't ransom you, to your folks, I might see what the fort'll give for ya.

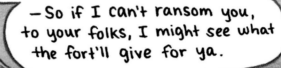

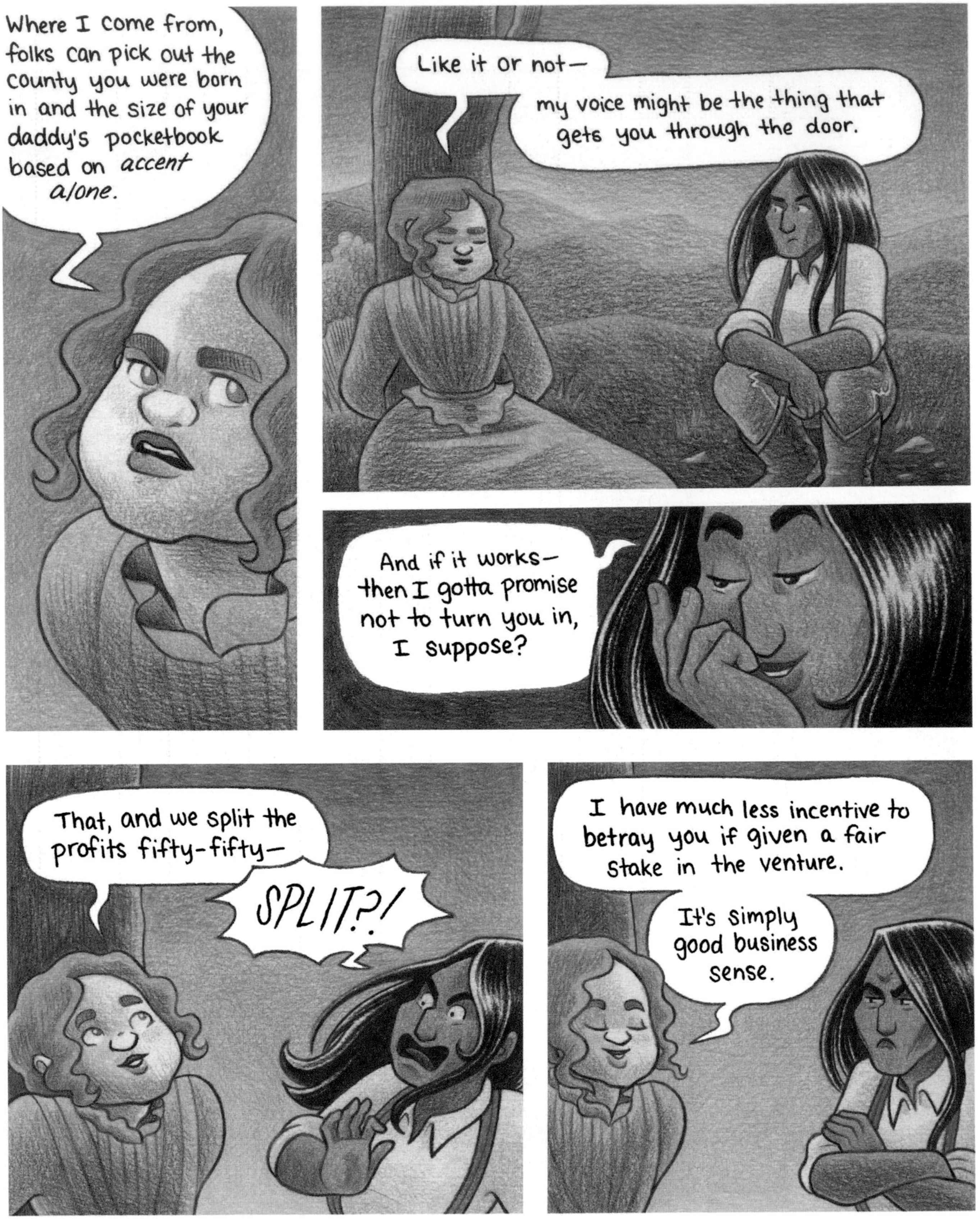
Where I come from, folks can pick out the county you were born in and the size of your daddy's pocketbook based on *accent alone*.
Like it or not—
my voice might be the thing that gets you through the door.
And if it works— then I gotta promise not to turn you in, I suppose?
That, and we split the profits fifty-fifty—
SPLIT?!
I have much less incentive to betray you if given a fair stake in the venture.
It's simply good business sense.

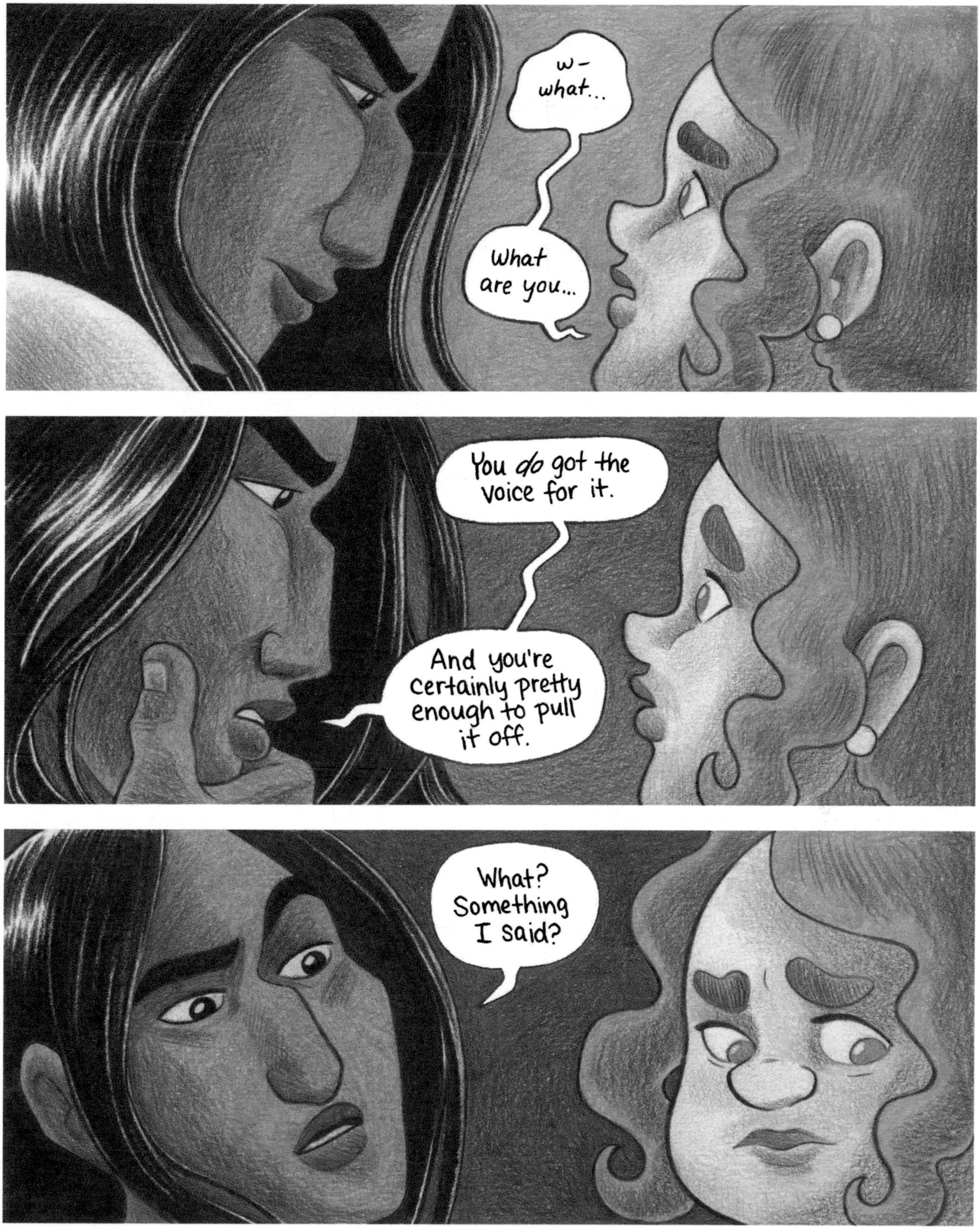
w- what...
What are you...
You *do* got the voice for it.
And you're certainly pretty enough to pull it off.
What? Something I said?

CHAPTER THREE

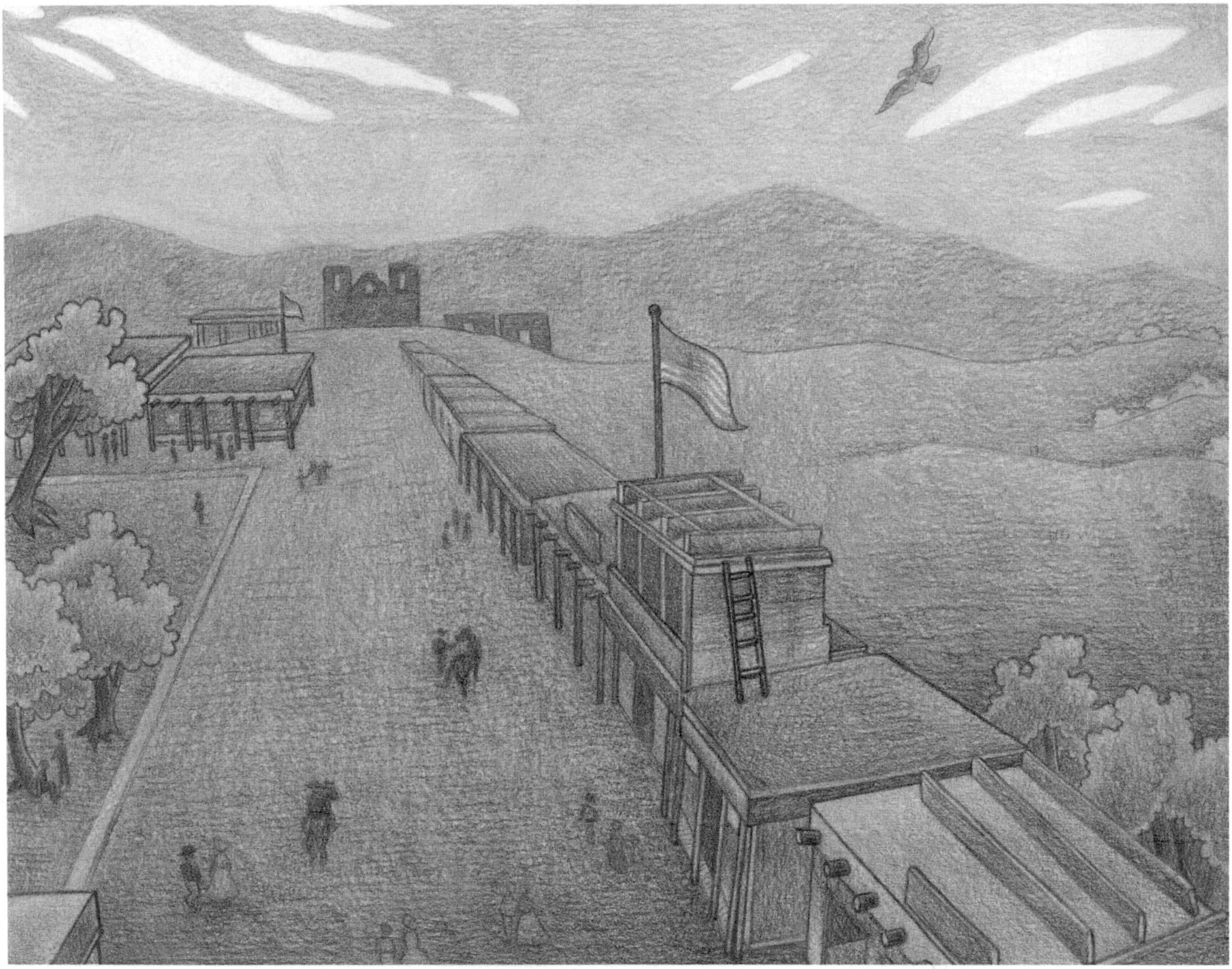

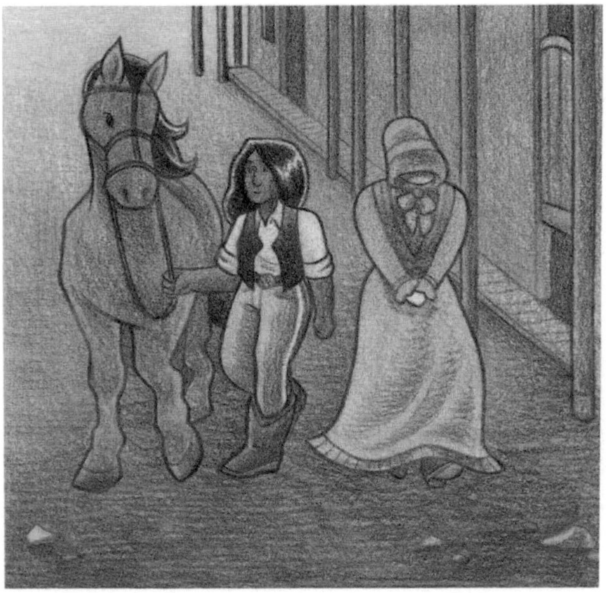

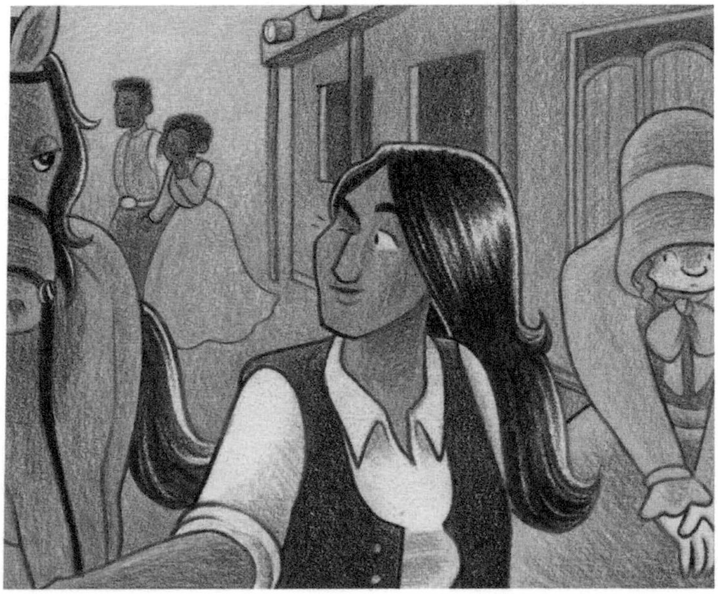

45

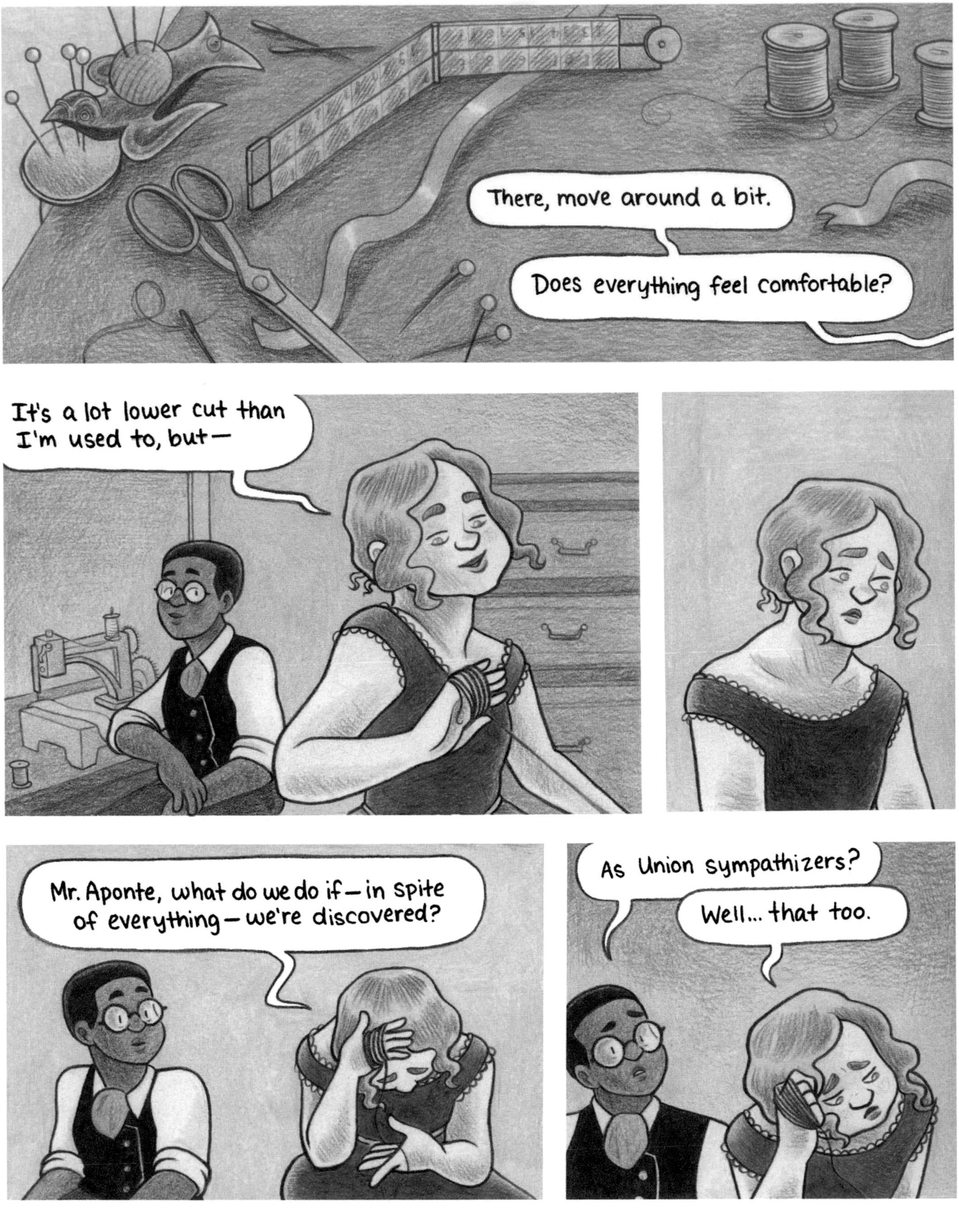
There, move around a bit.
Does everything feel comfortable?
It's a lot lower cut than I'm used to, but—
Mr. Aponte, what do we do if—in spite of everything—we're discovered?
As Union sympathizers?
Well... that too.

CHAPTER FOUR

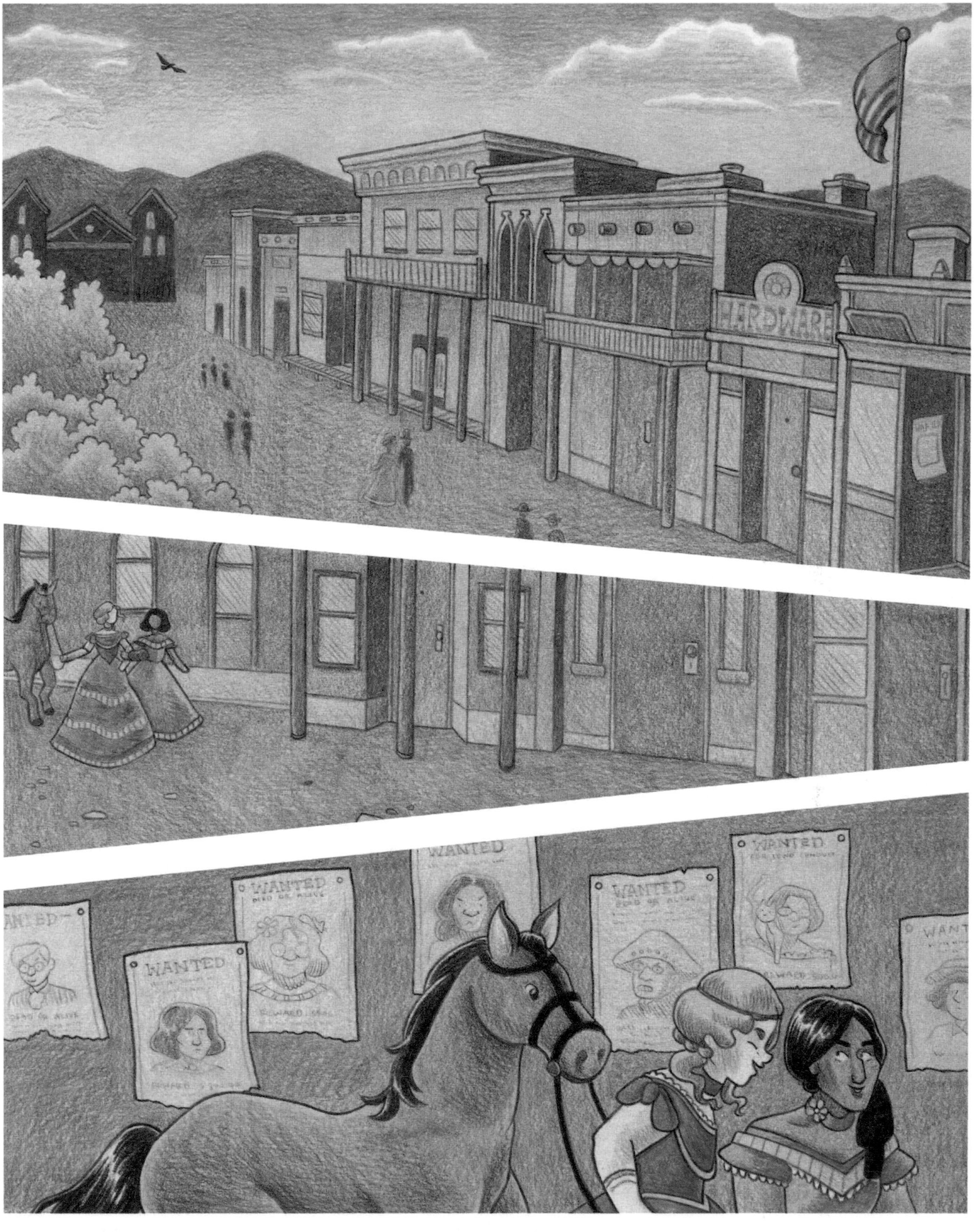
HARDWARE
WANTED
WANTED
WANTED
WANTED
WANTED

56

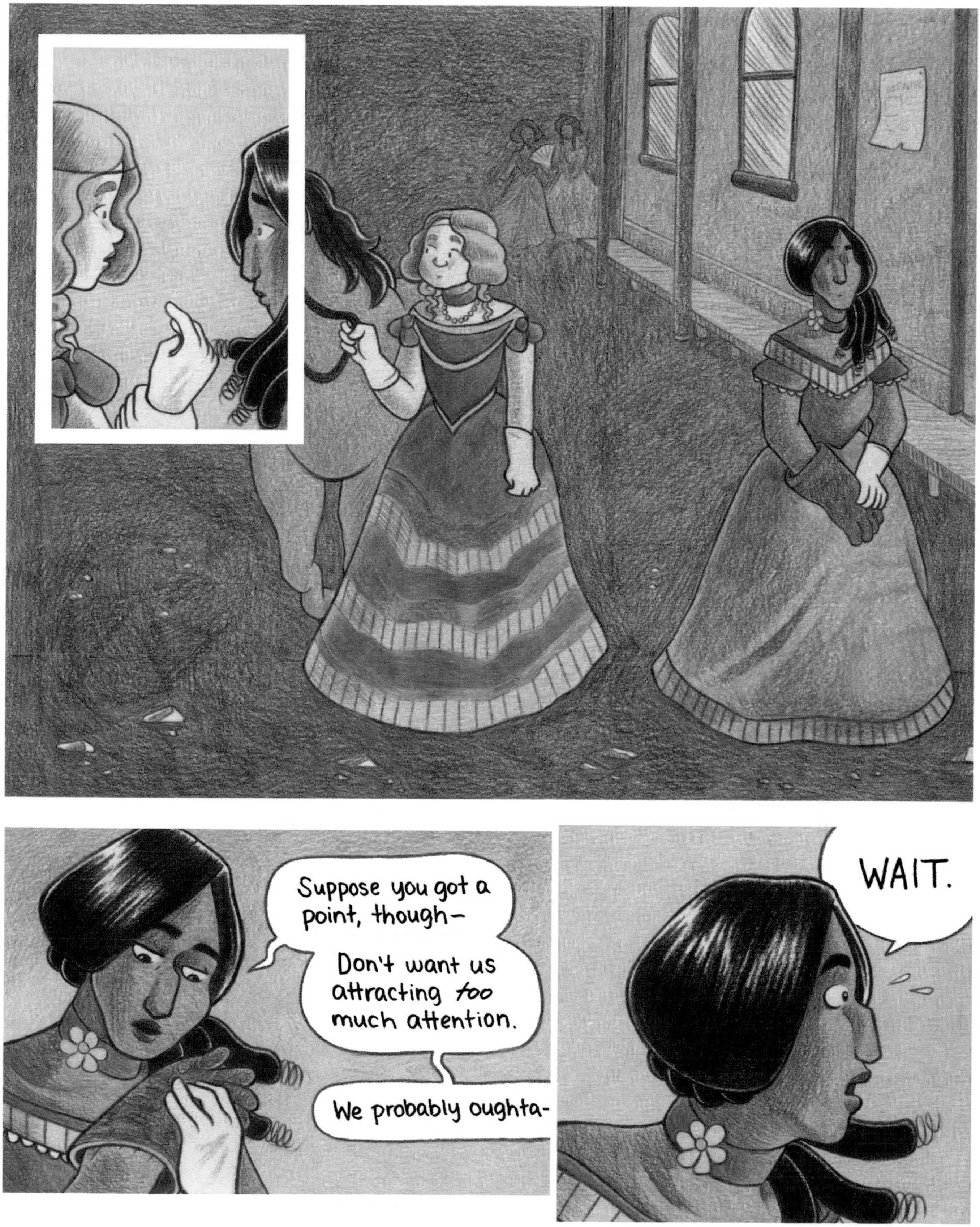
Suppose you got a point, though–
Don't want us attracting *too* much attention.
We probably oughta-
WAIT.

58

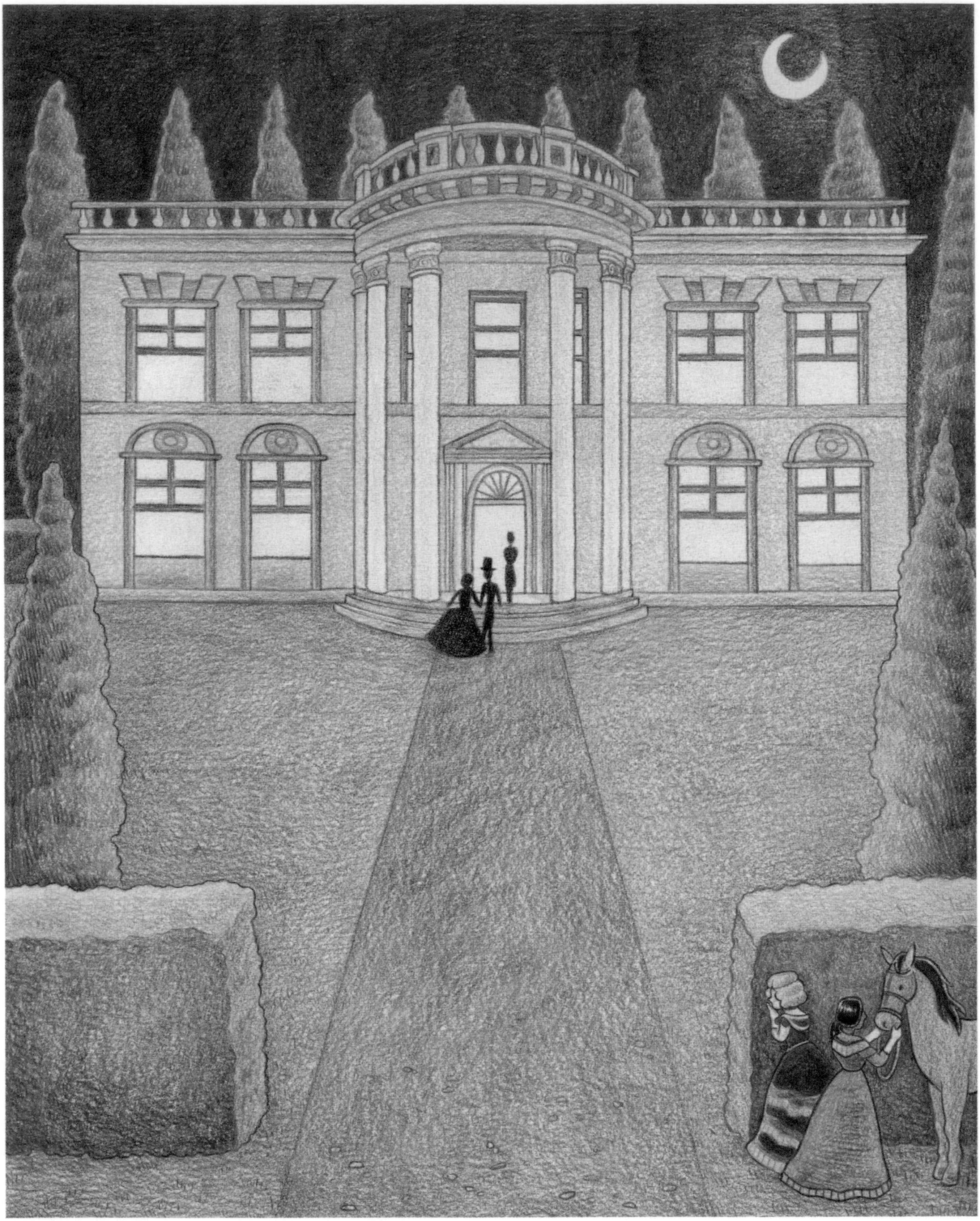

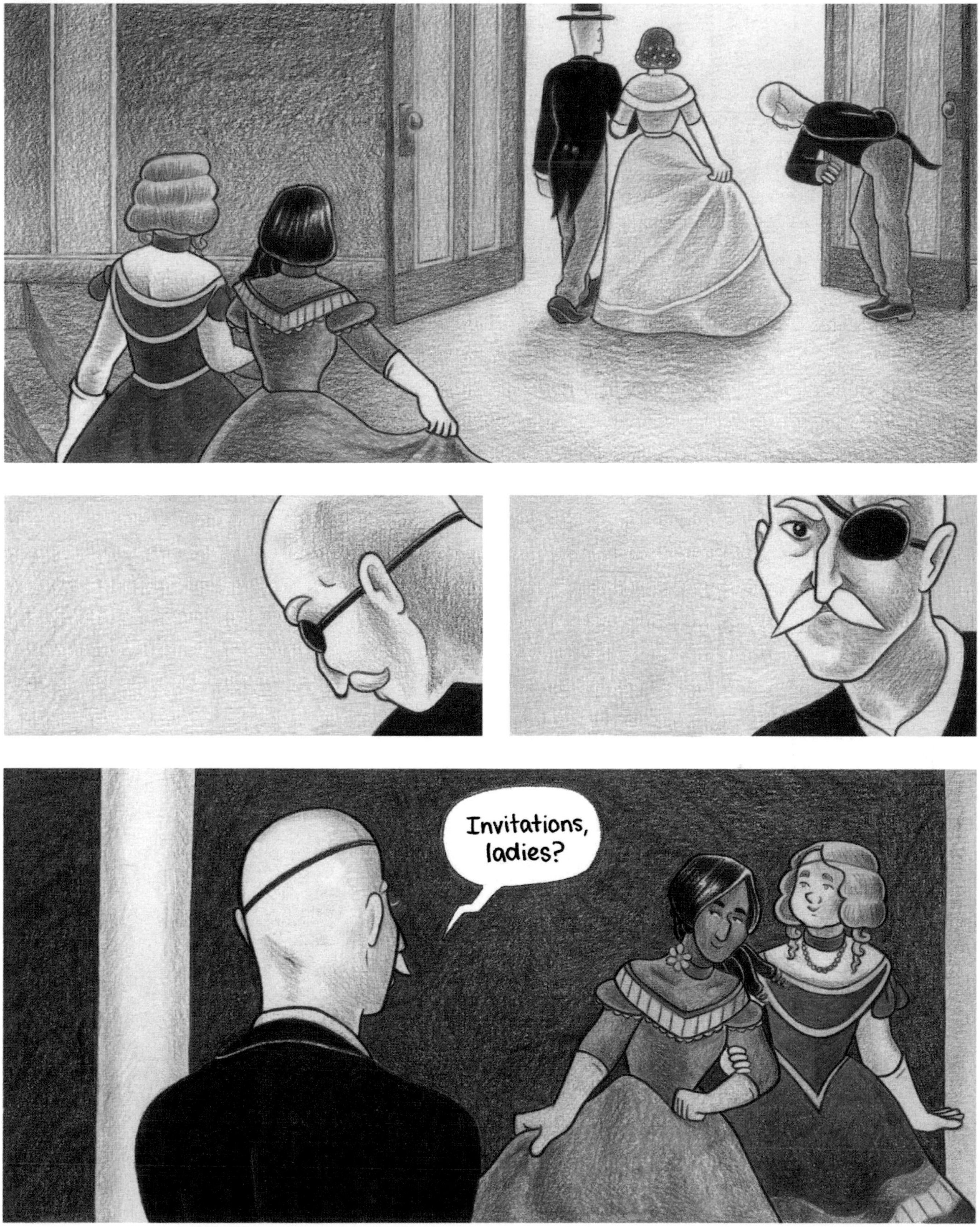
Invitations, ladies?

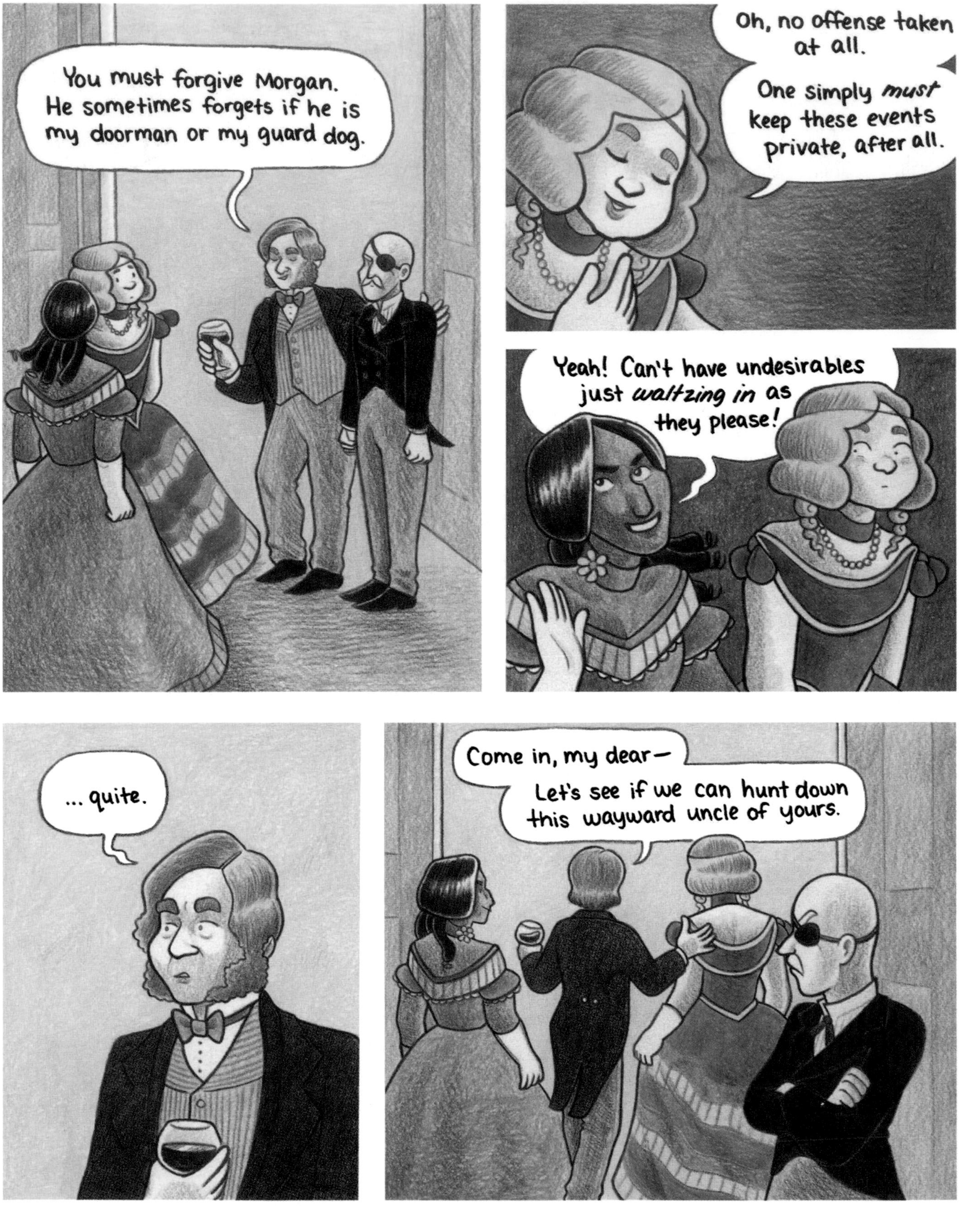
You must forgive Morgan. He sometimes forgets if he is my doorman or my guard dog.
Oh, no offense taken at all.
One simply *must* keep these events private, after all.
Yeah! Can't have undesirables just *waltzing in* as they please!
... quite.
Come in, my dear—
Let's see if we can hunt down this wayward uncle of yours.

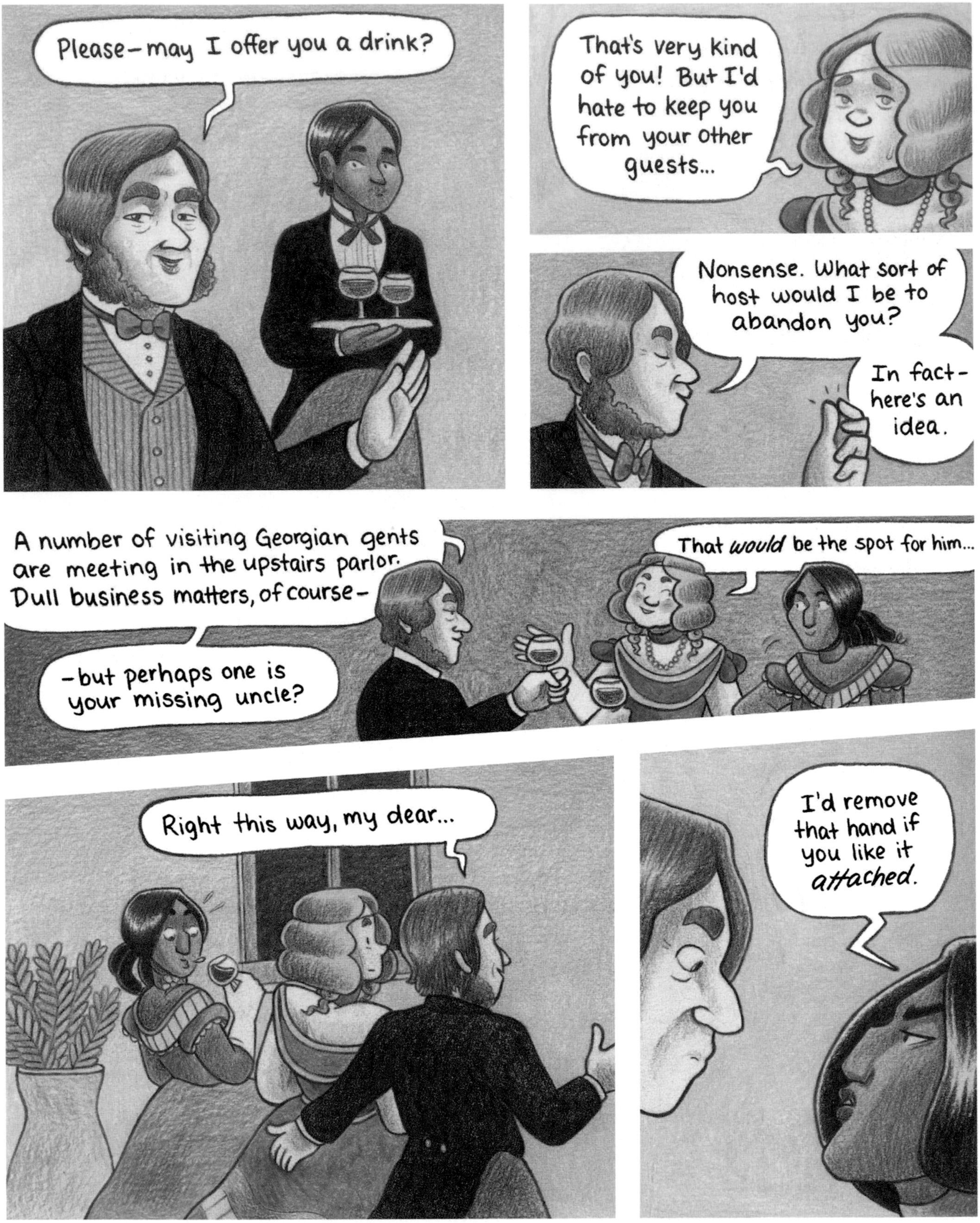
Please—may I offer you a drink?
That's very kind of you! But I'd hate to keep you from your other guests...
Nonsense. What sort of host would I be to abandon you?
In fact—here's an idea.
A number of visiting Georgian gents are meeting in the upstairs parlor. Dull business matters, of course—
—but perhaps one is your missing uncle?
That *would* be the spot for him...
Right this way, my dear...
I'd remove that hand if you like it *attached*.

CHAPTER FIVE

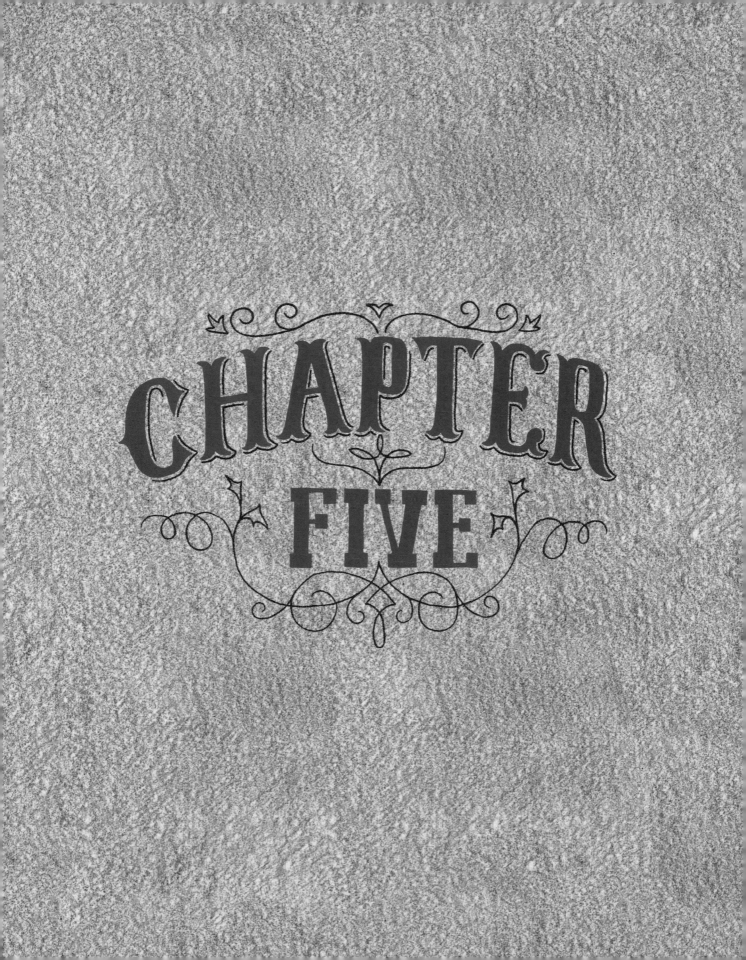

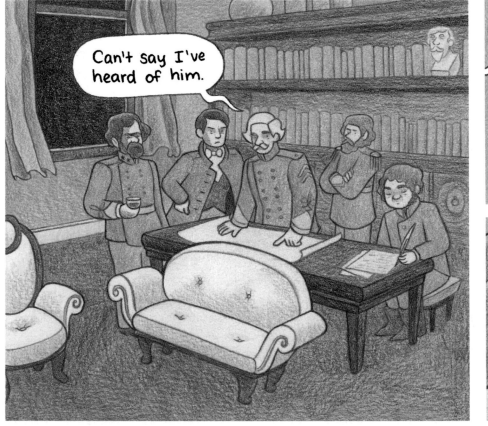

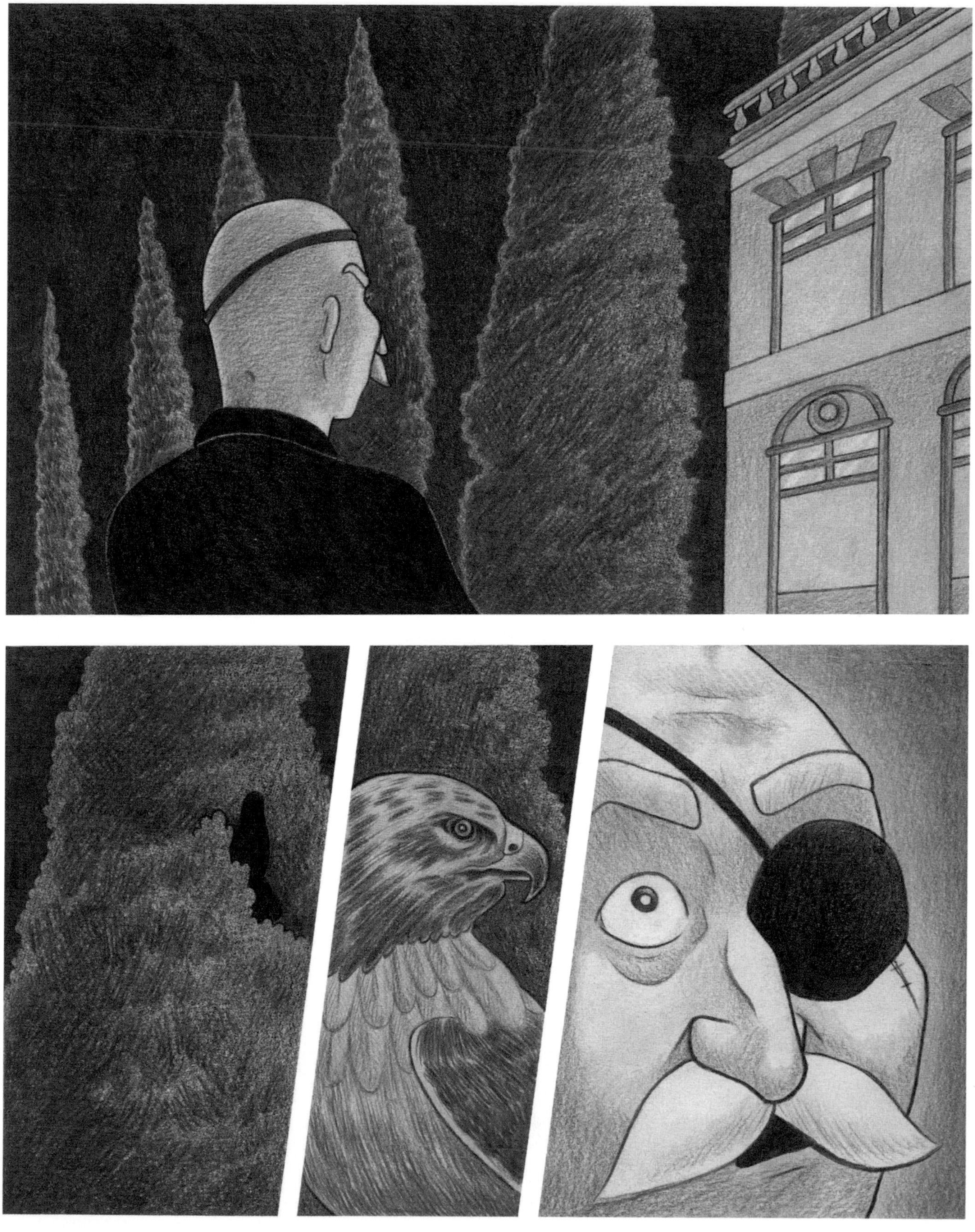

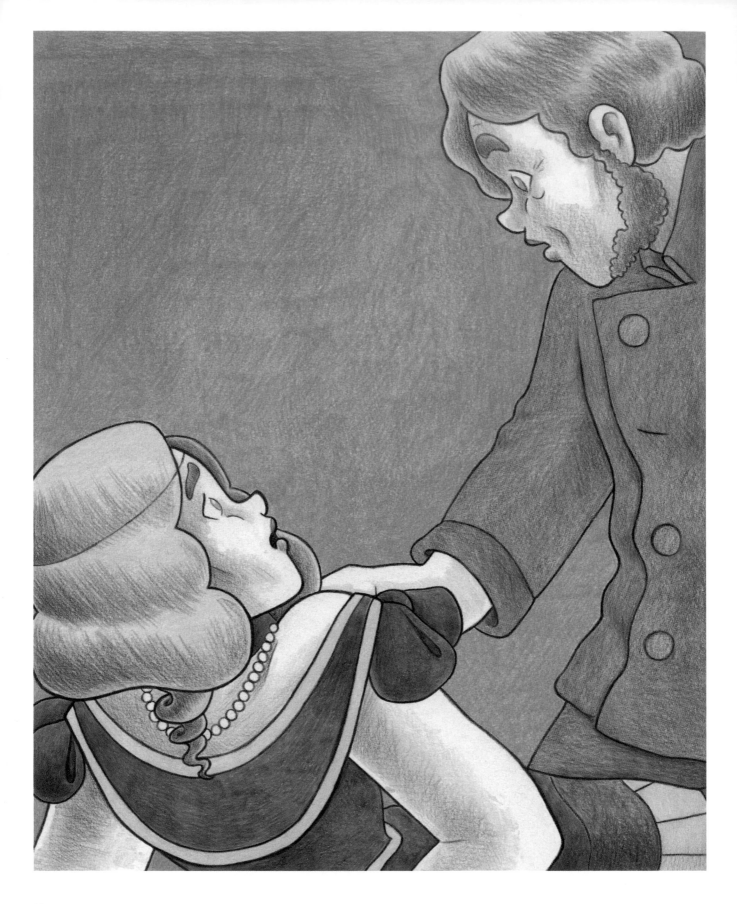

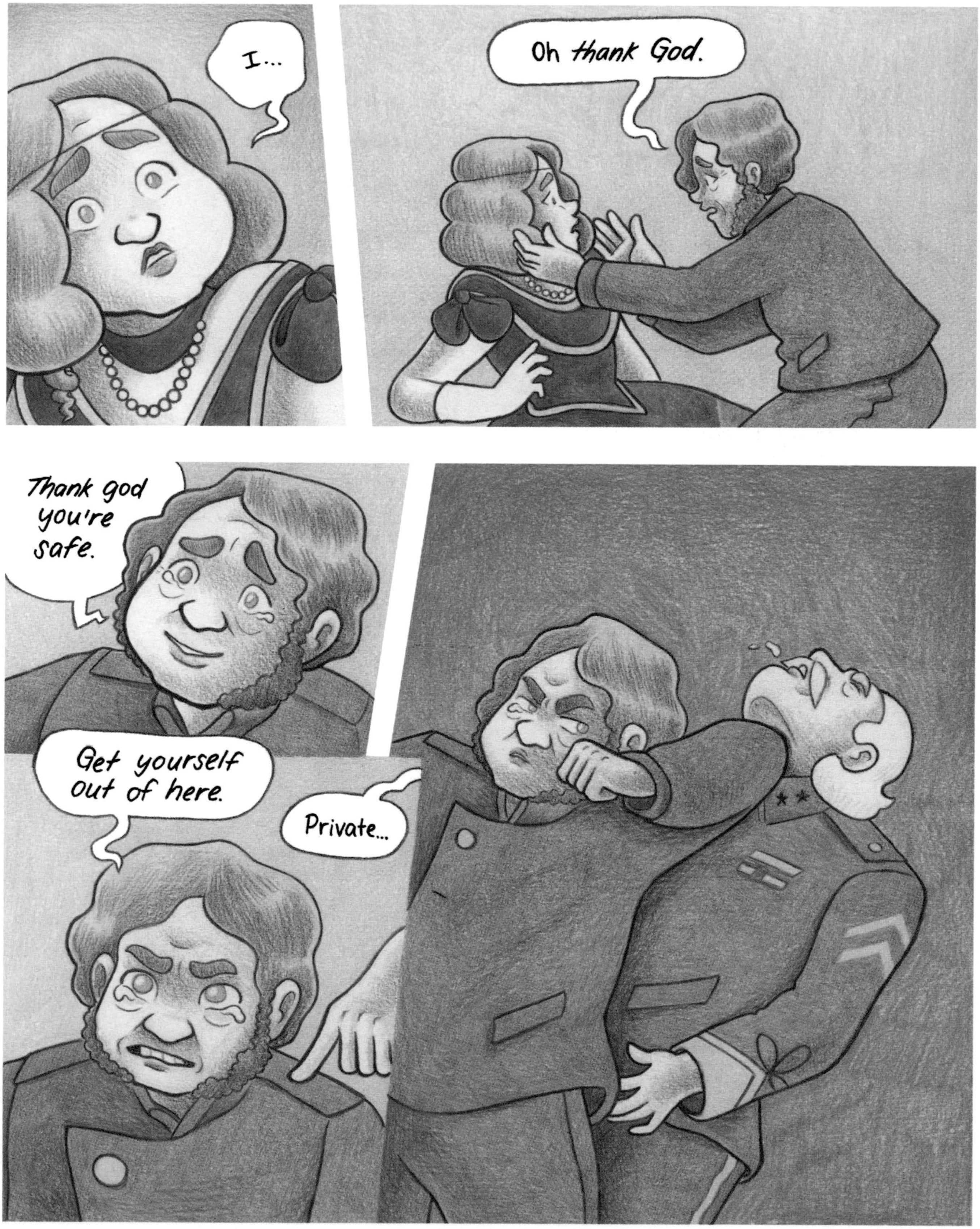
I...
Oh thank God.
Thank god you're safe.
Get yourself out of here.
Private...

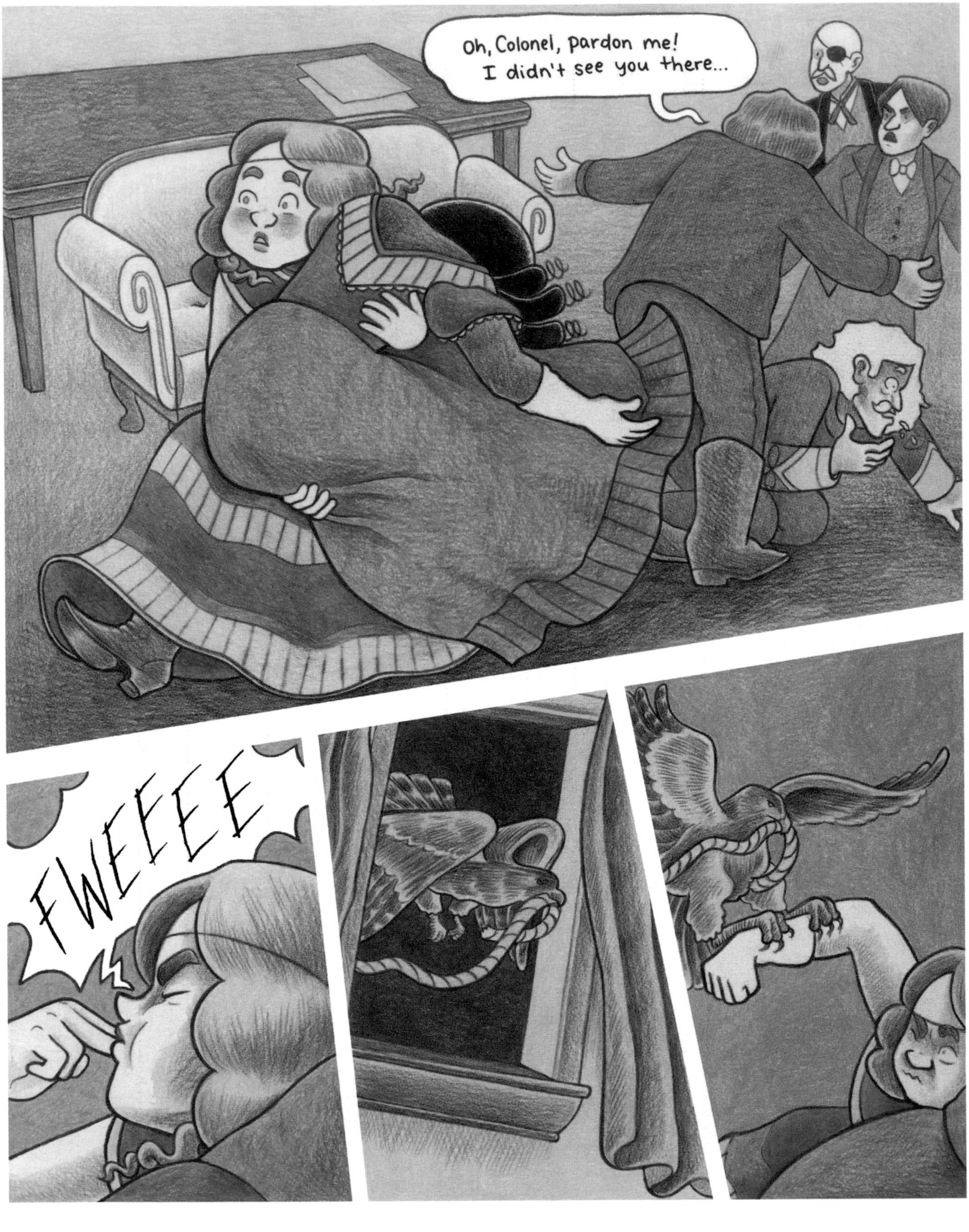
Oh, Colonel, pardon me! I didn't see you there...
FWEEEE

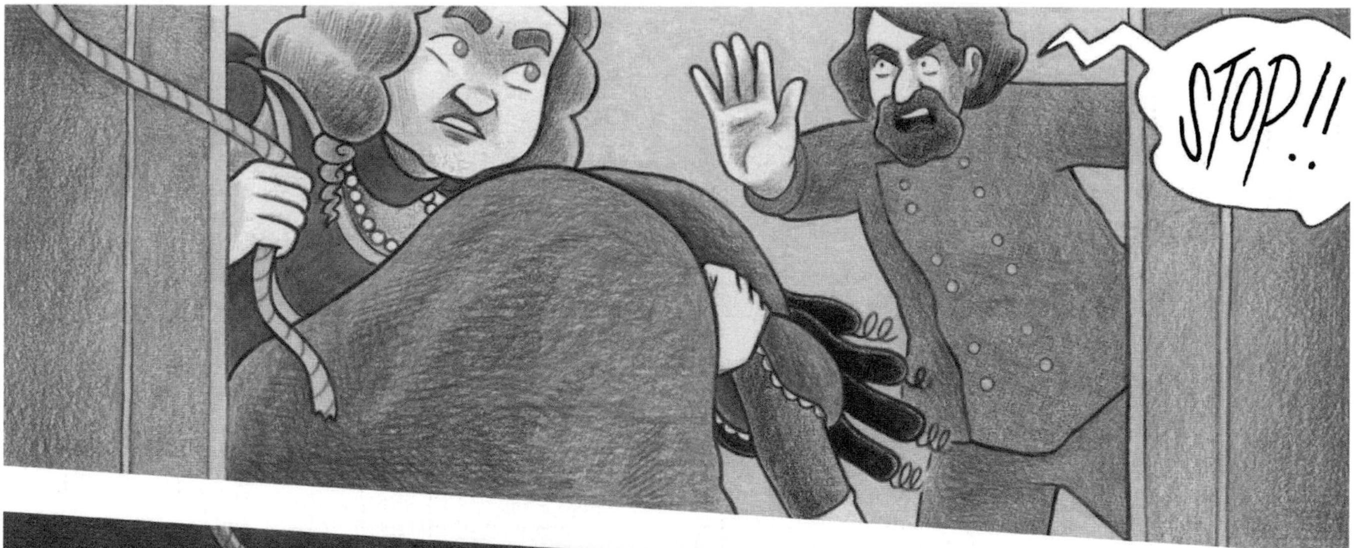
STOP!!

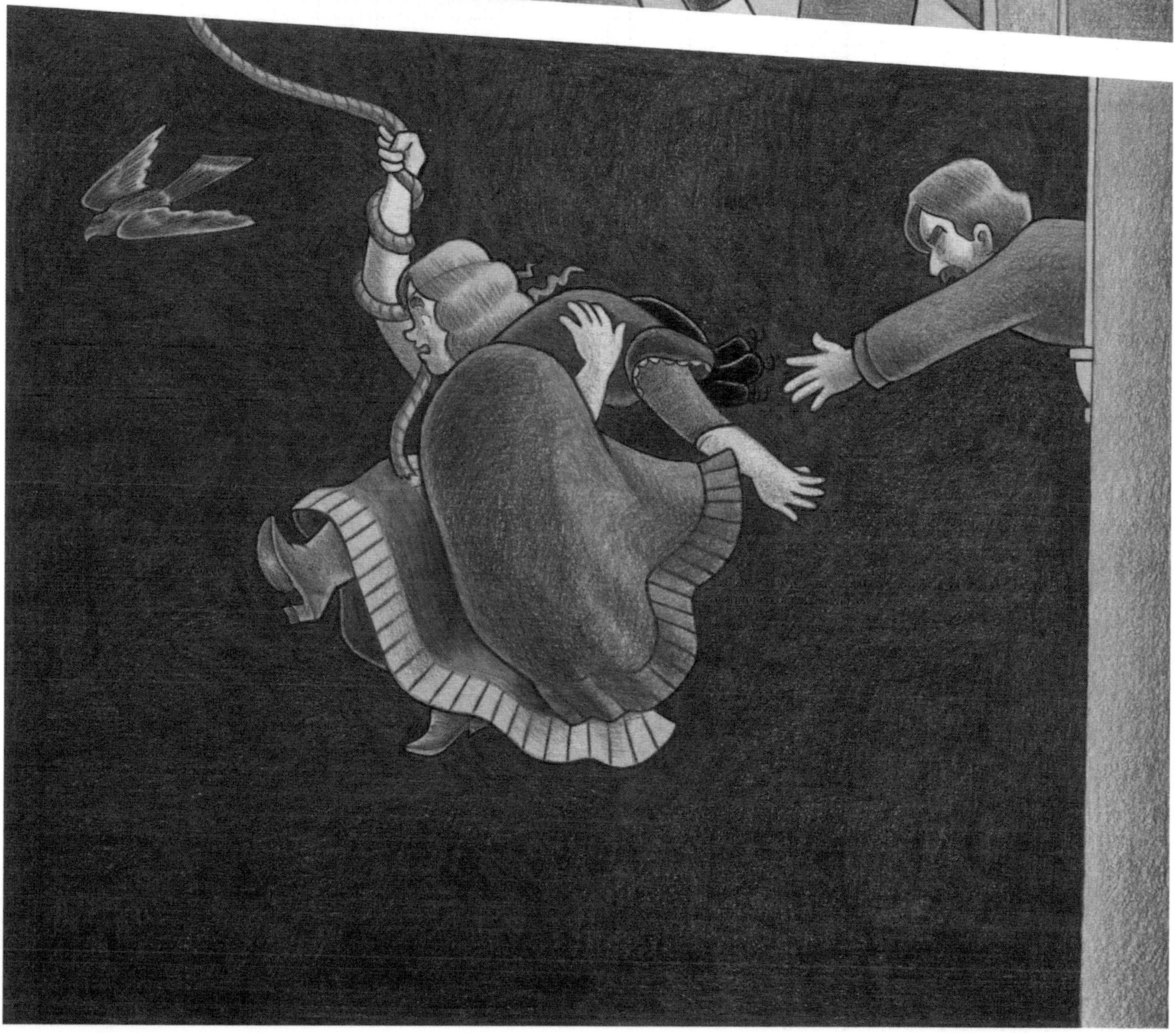

CHAPTER SIX

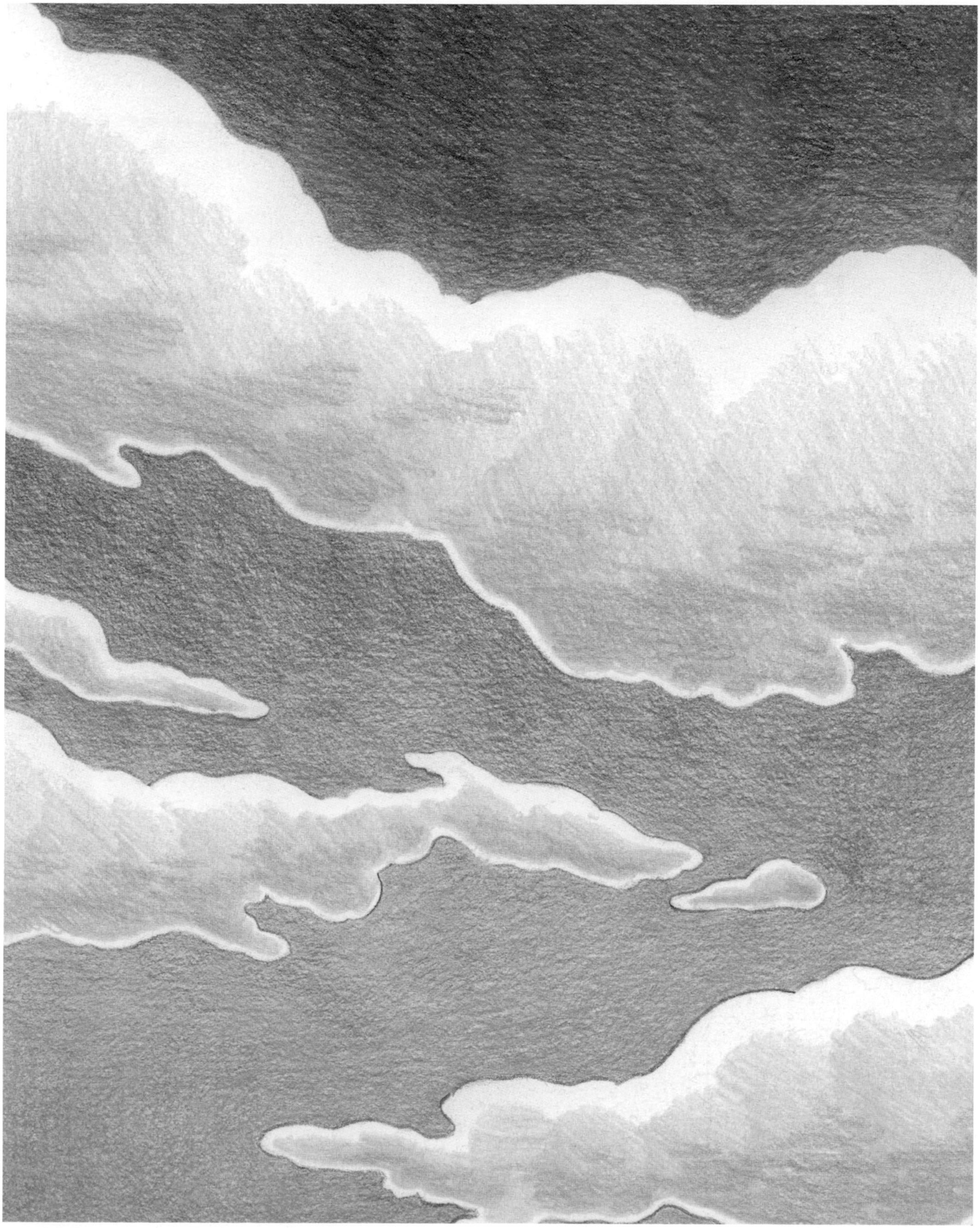

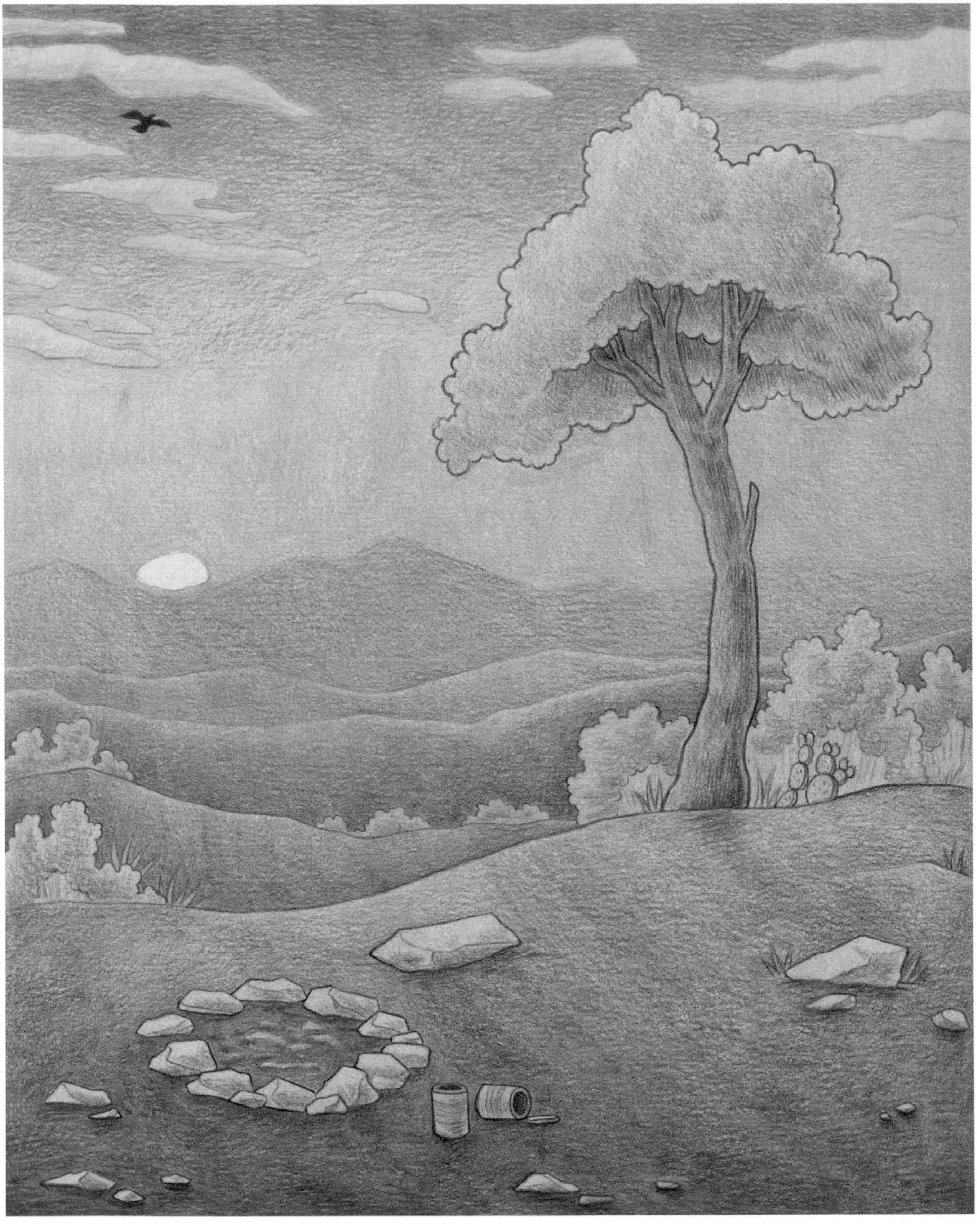

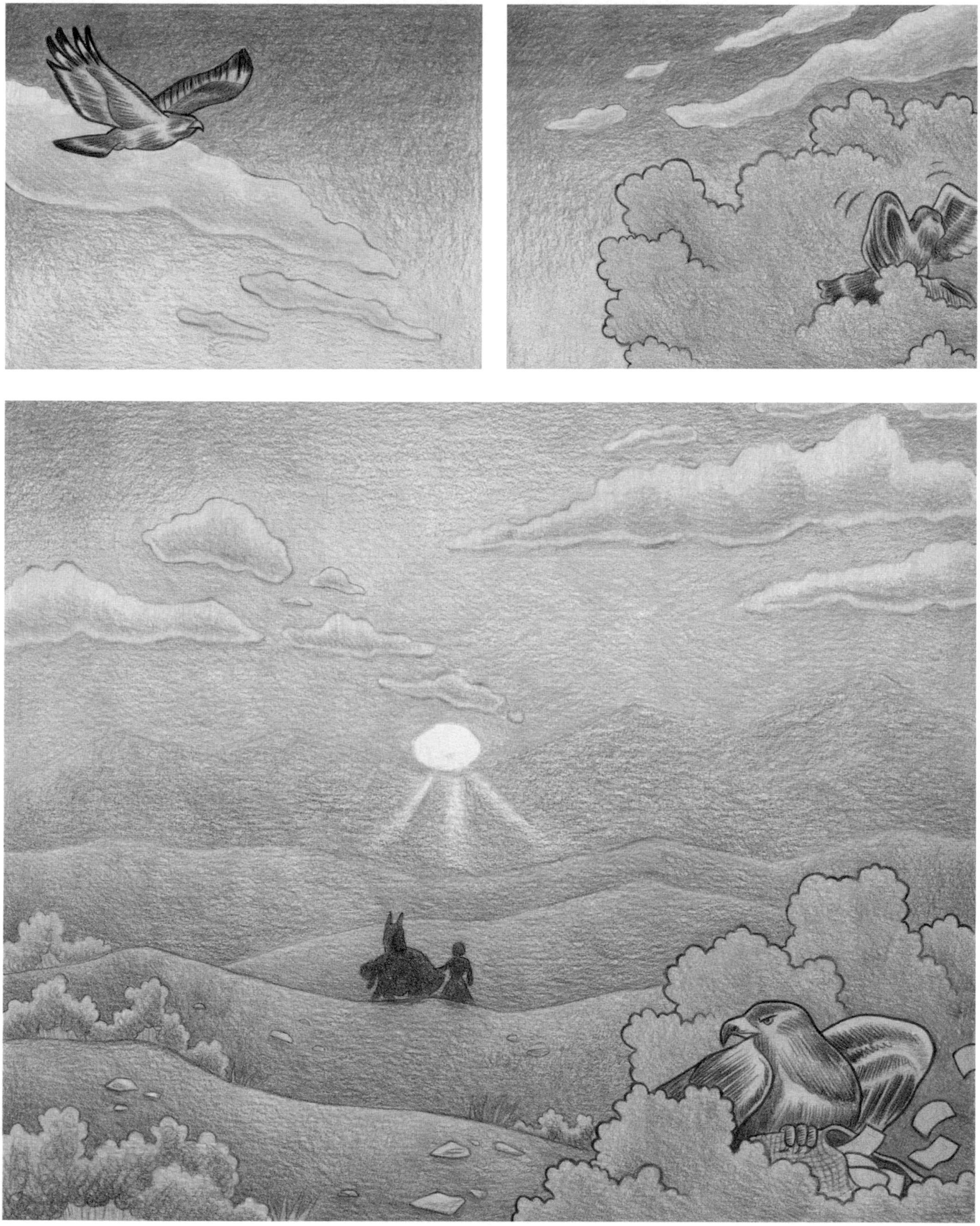

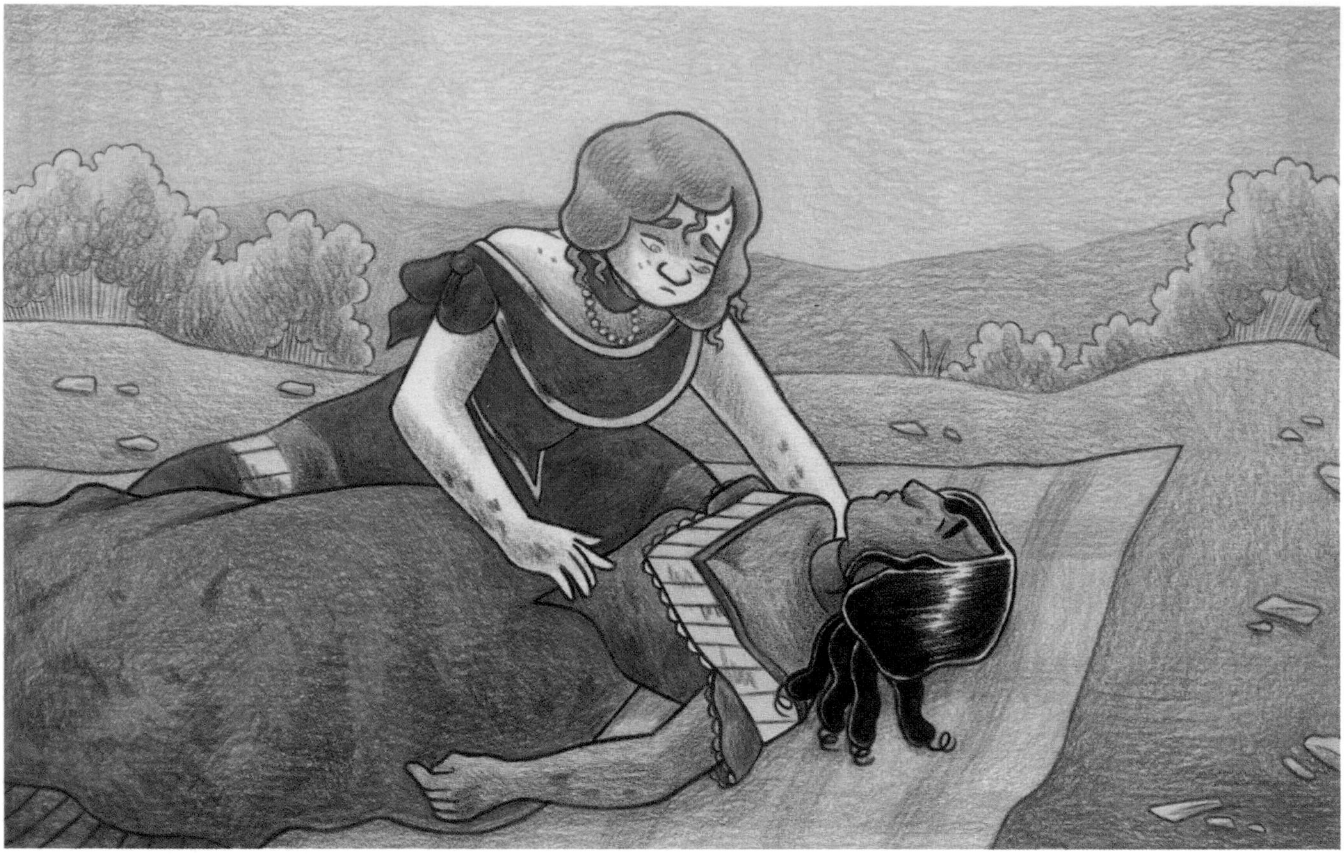

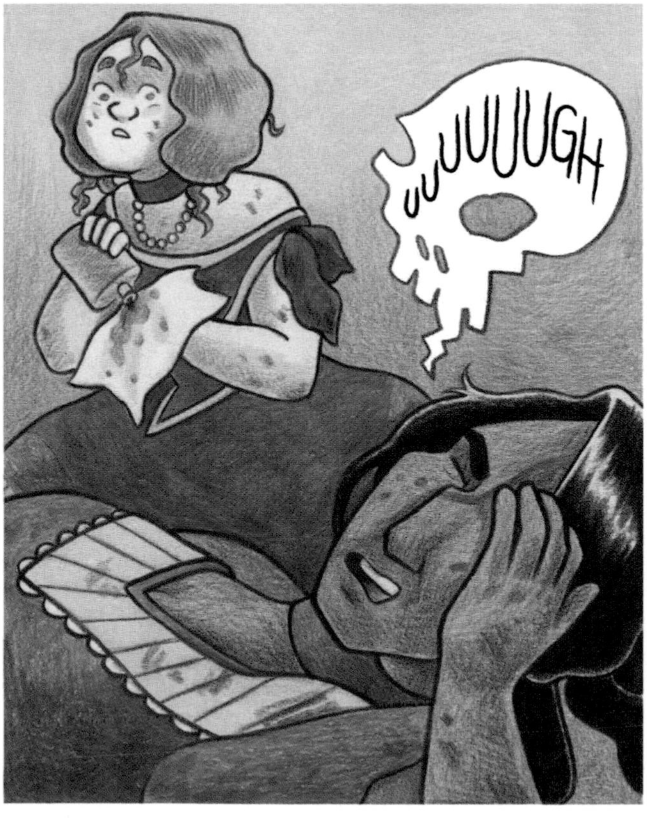
uuUUUUGH

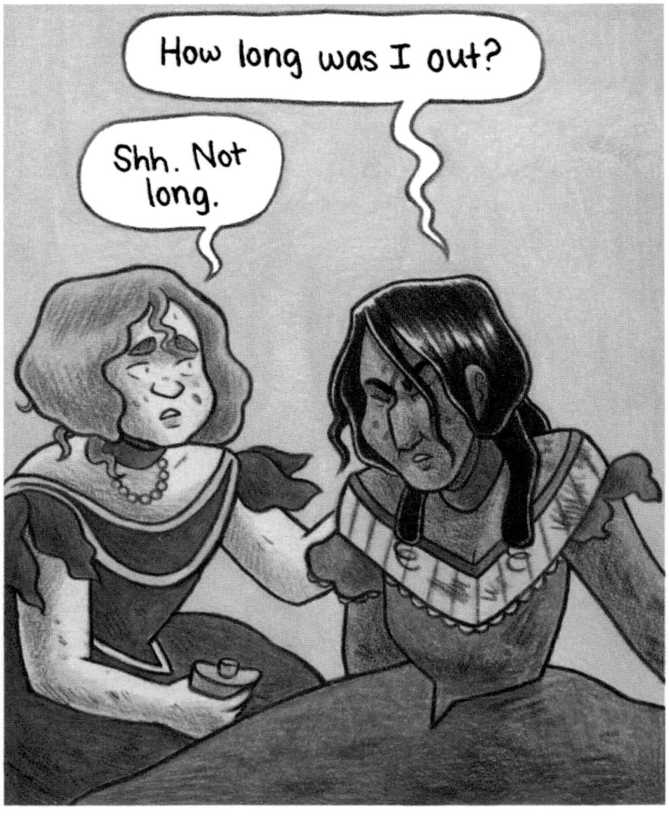
How long was I out?
Shh. Not long.

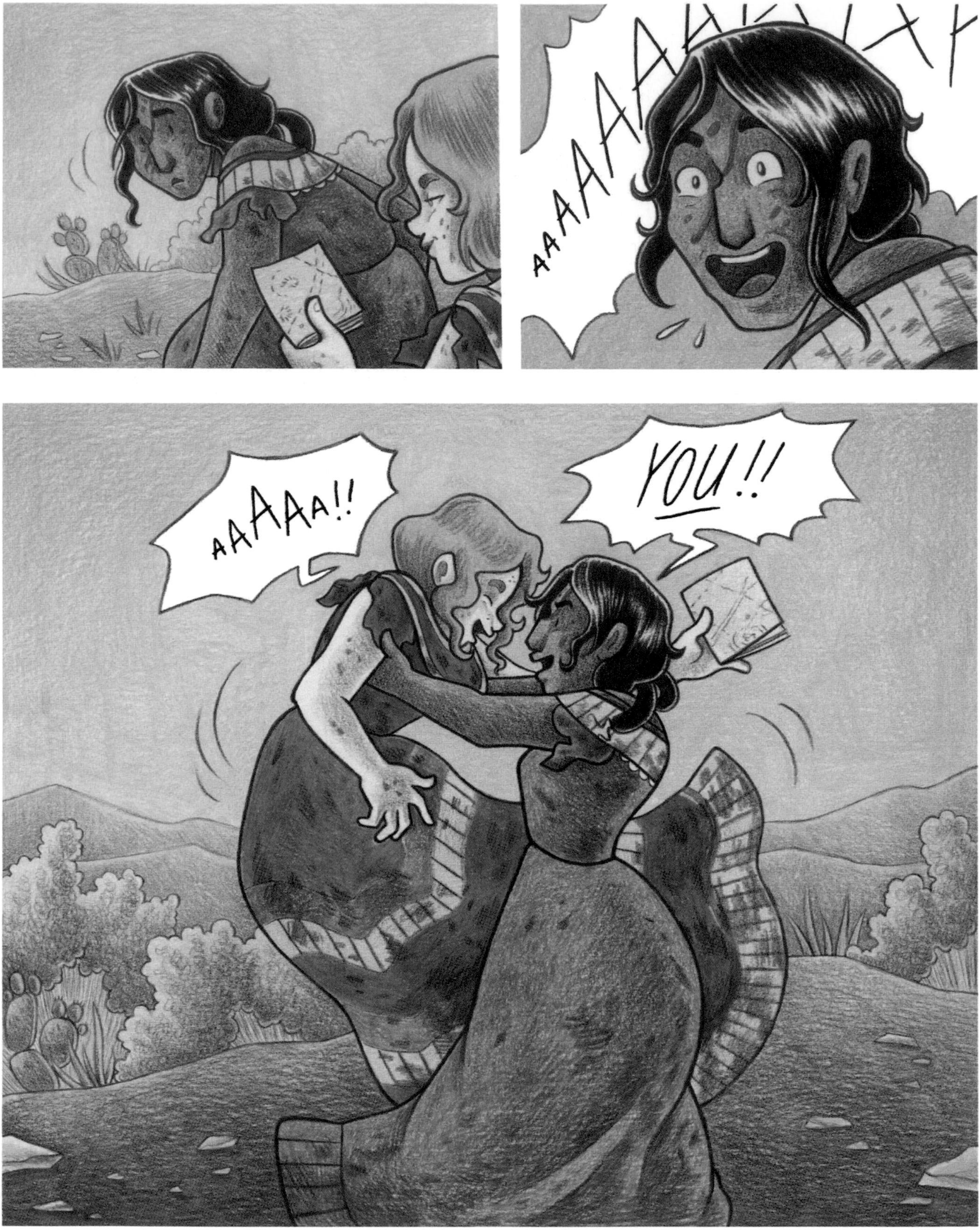
AAAAAAA
AAAAa!!
YOU!!

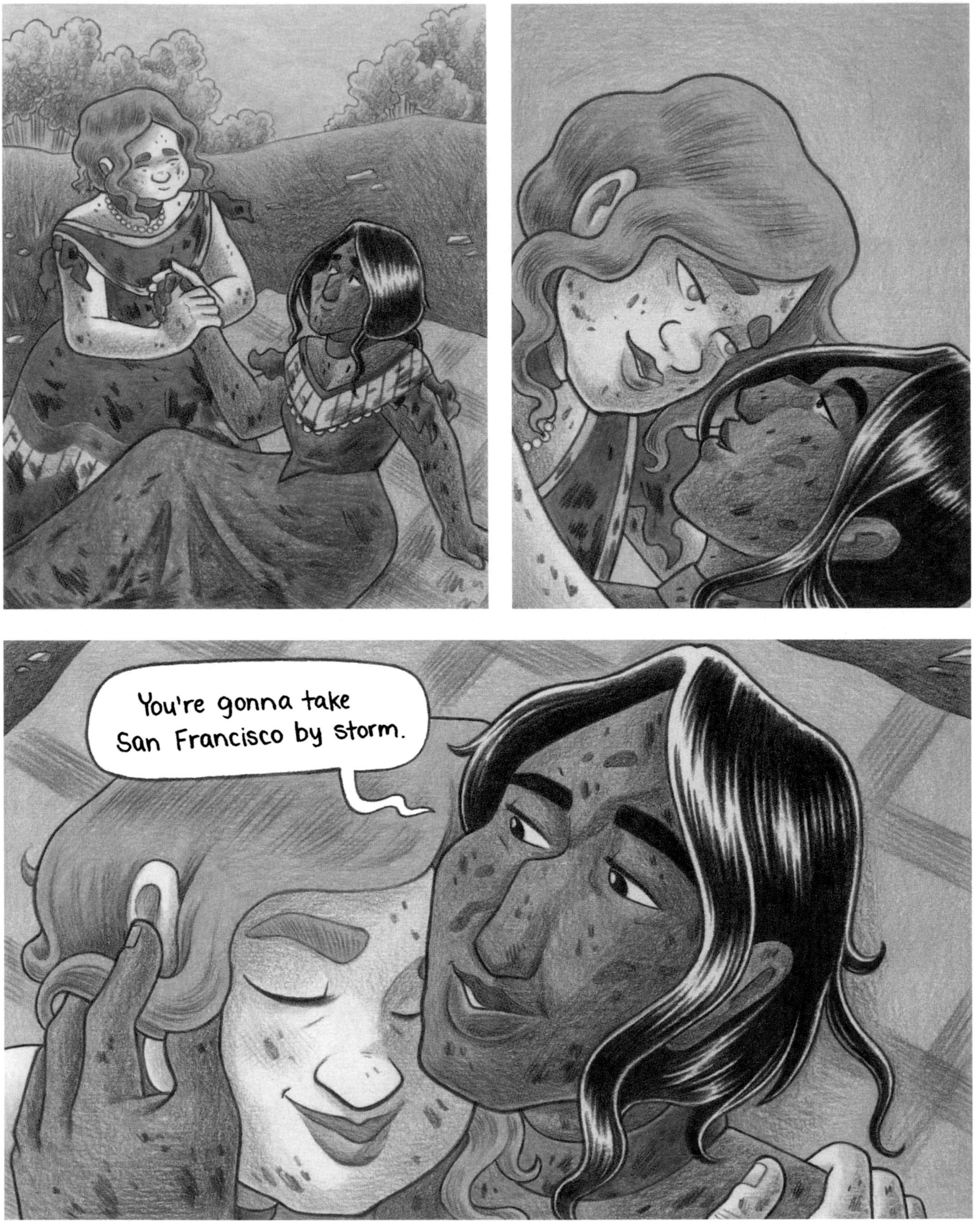
You're gonna take San Francisco by storm.

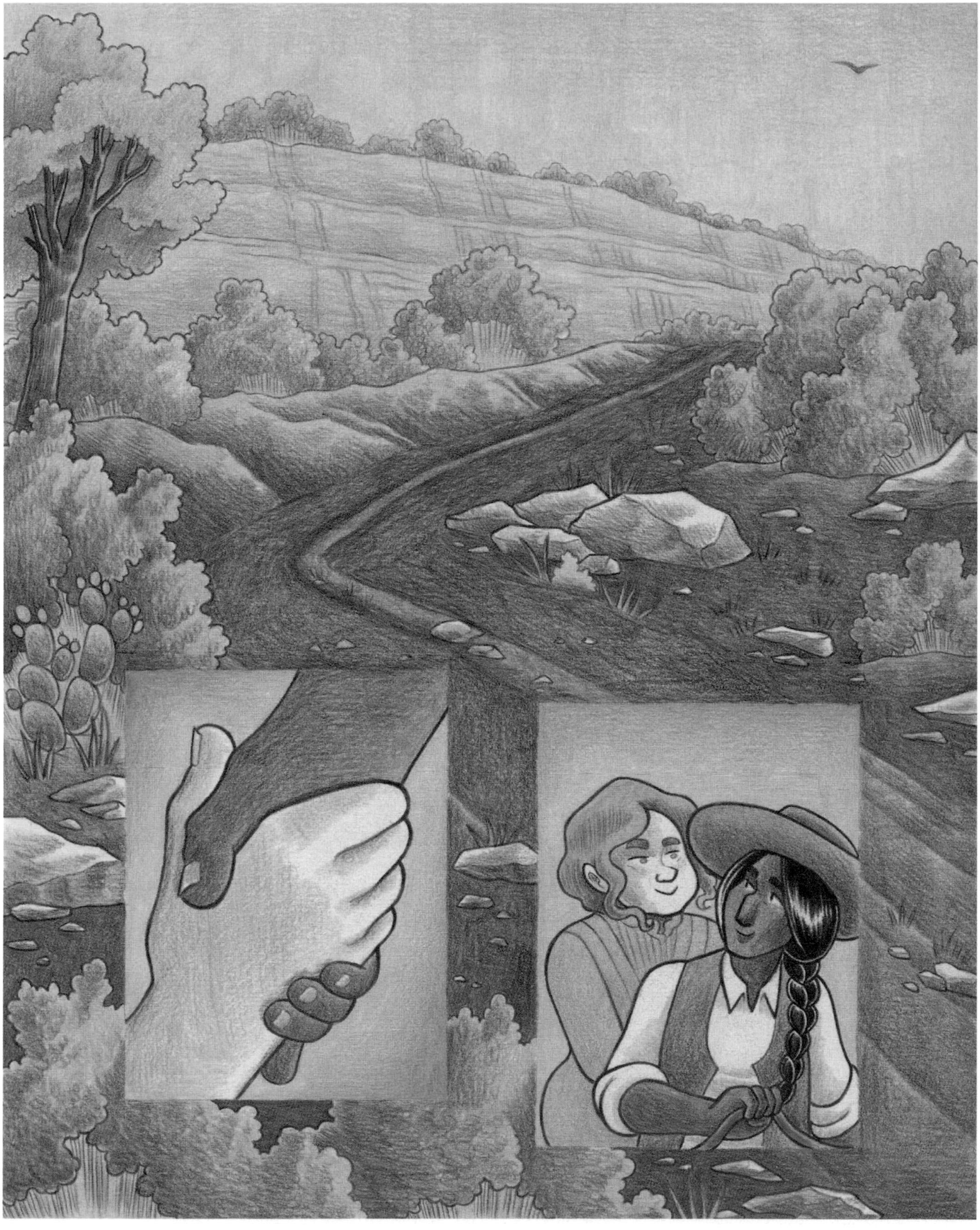

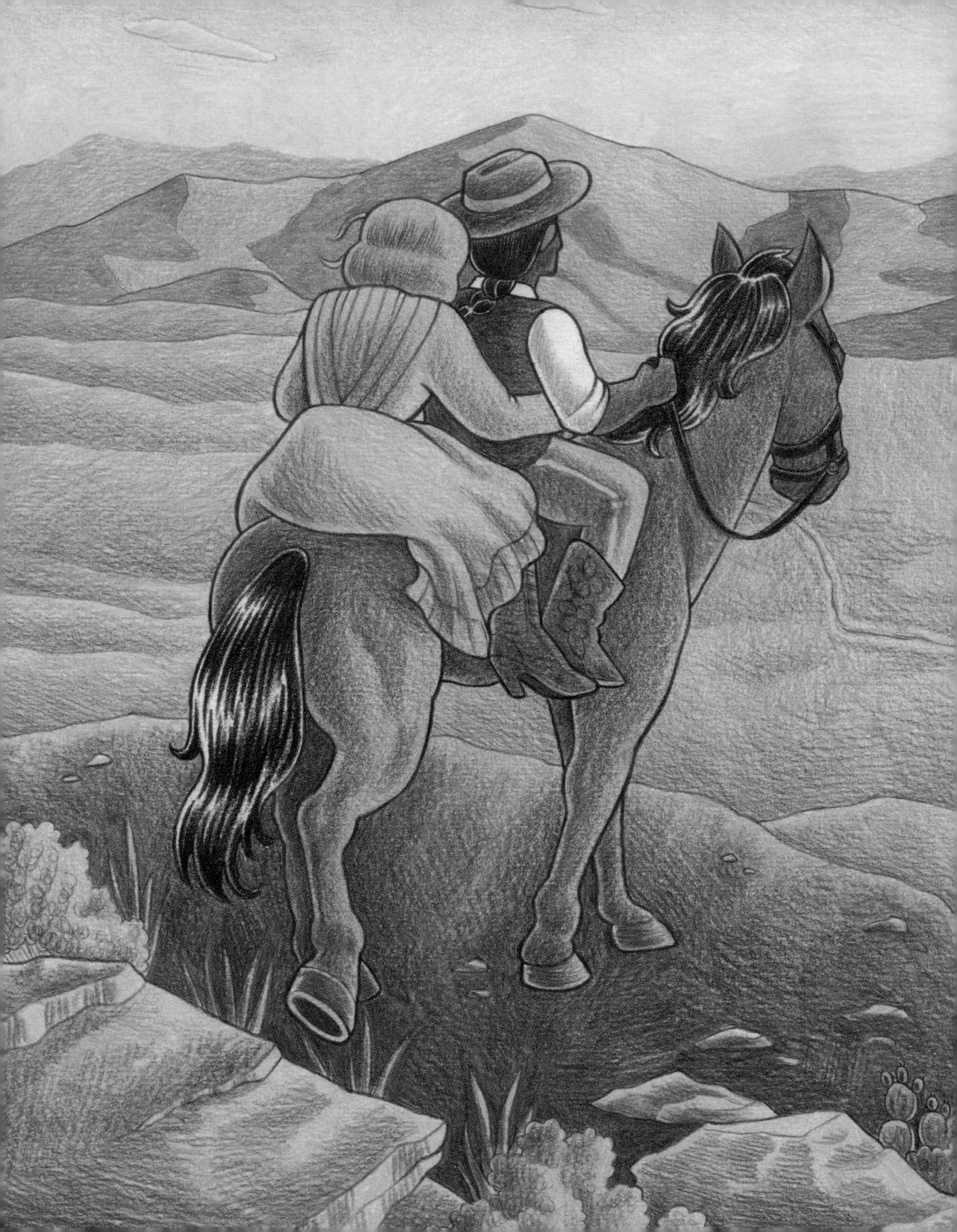

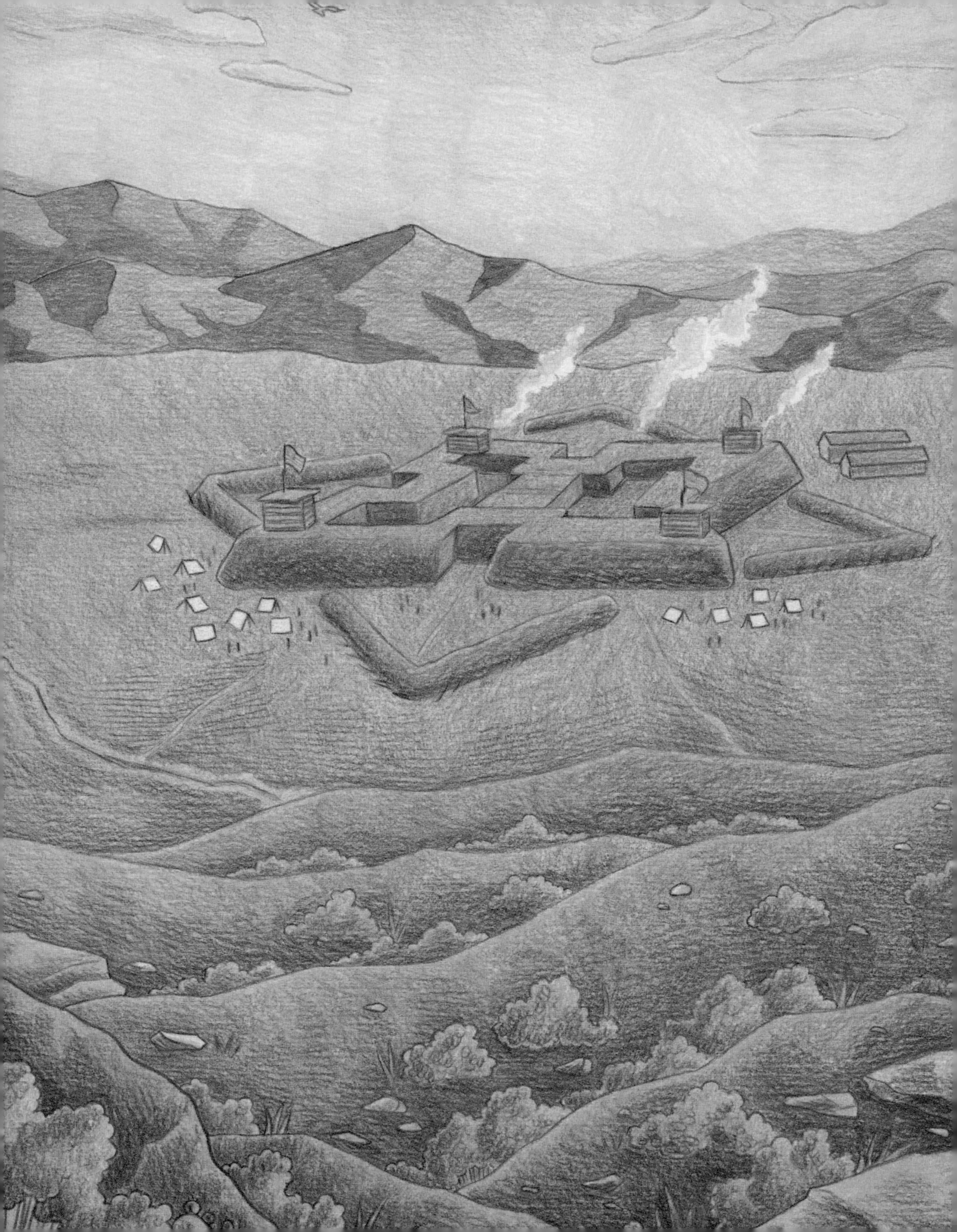

Stage Dreams, Annotated

Page 9

In 1861, New Mexico Territory was still part of the Union (the United States of America), at least on paper. New Mexicans were divided about the Civil War—many people supported the Union, many people supported the Confederacy, and many people thought New Mexico should have nothing whatsoever to do with a war happening on the other side of the country. New Mexico was about to get dragged into the war whether it liked it or not, though. In July 1861, Confederate troops managed to take over the southern half of the territory. They renamed it the Confederate Territory of Arizona. Soon after, Confederate brigadier general Henry Hopkins Sibley began making plans to advance into the northern half of the territory, with hopes he could take over Albuquerque, Santa Fe, and the gold mines of Colorado en route to California.

Page 16

The strongbox here is filled with demand notes—the first paper money to achieve wide circulation in the United States. The US Treasury first printed demand notes in August 1861. Prior to the Civil War, US dollars were all coins minted from precious metals such as gold and silver; unlike paper money, the coins had inherent value. Paper money was controversial and unpopular when it first debuted in the United States, because people didn't trust that pieces of paper would keep their value over time! You can imagine how frustrating this would be for an outlaw in 1861, robbing a stagecoach and hoping to find it full of gold, only to end up with a chest full of nothing but paper.

Page 22

Despite how frequently they're erased from history books, we can still find a handful of records of transgender people living in early American history! The total number of surviving pre-twentieth century records is relatively small, but that doesn't mean there weren't many trans people at the time. More likely, few records exist because trans people were forced to live stealthily throughout most of US history. Surviving accounts of historical trans people were usually only written if the person in question was publicly outed—often by law enforcement, medical professionals, or coroners after the person's death.

Mary Jones was a Black trans sex worker who was put on trial in New York in 1836 after she pickpocketed a few of her clients; her trial became a public scandal in part because she was trans. Mrs. Nash, a trans cook and laundress, worked for Lieutenant Colonel George Armstrong Custer's 7th Cavalry just a few years before the Battle of Little Bighorn. She also married three different men in the course of her lifetime. Her trans identity wasn't discovered until after her death.

Hundreds of AFAB (assigned female at birth) people dressed as men to enlist in the army on both sides of the Civil War. While not all of them were trans, there are a few accounts of veterans who continued to live as men for the rest of their lives, including Albert Cashier, a member of the 95th Illinois Infantry Regiment. Other examples of trans men in the American West include Mountain Charley (a one-eyed stagecoach driver and famed crack shot with a pistol) and Harry Allen (an outlaw and a rare example of an out trans man in the nineteeth century). Many Indigenous nations in the West also included two-spirit people, such as We'wha, a famous mediator and member of the Zuni tribe. We'wha lived in New Mexico in the latter half of the nineteeth century. Most likely, there are thousands of other historical trans Americans whose names we will never know, either because their records were lost or erased or because they managed to keep their trans identity a secret throughout their life.

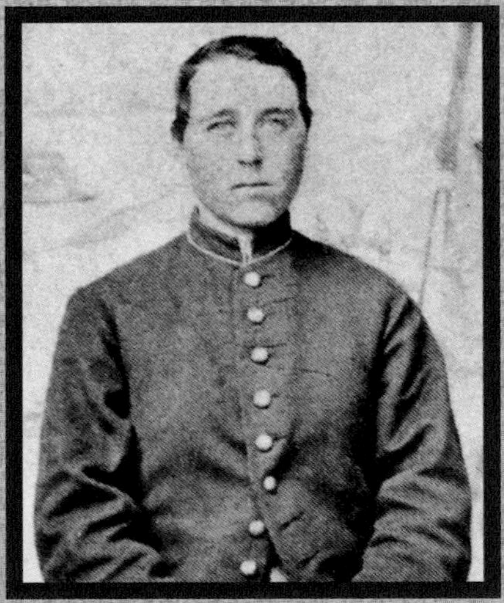

Albert Cashier, a trans man who served in the 95th Illinois Infantry Regiment during the US Civil War.

Page 24

Grace says she wants to avoid "conscription," but the Confederate army didn't officially institute a draft until April 1862. In my mind, Grace is using the word that best describes the sense of entrapment she feels. In the South, community expectations, family obligations, and financial destitution would all be strong forces pushing her to enlist, draft or no draft. Running away was her best option to avoid military service.

Page 25

"Rich man's war, poor man's fight" was a common complaint of low-income people on both sides of the Civil War. In the South, many poor white people viewed the war as something they would be forced to die for but which would only benefit the interests of the land- and slave-owning rich. However, this anti-war stance does not excuse poor white Southerners from racism—even if they were against the war, the vast majority of them were still pro-slavery. I included this detail in the book in part because numerous contemporary writers and historians, in their attempts to romanticize the Confederacy, often gloss it over. Promoting a historical image of Southerners as uniformly eager to fight and die in the war makes it easier to, for instance, defend Confederate monuments or pretend the Confederate flag represents nothing except "Southern heritage."

Page 29

Flor is alluding to a cross-country railroad line here! In 1861, the Union navy was blockading all Confederate ports in the Atlantic—which posed a huge problem for the South, the economy of which relied on trade with Europe. The Confederacy desperately needed gold and ports, so taking over the West and building a transcontinental rail line to the California coast would have given it a huge advantage in the war.

Page 30

Even though it hadn't happened yet, the Union army knew the Confederate army was planning to invade the northern half of New Mexico Territory. Given the relative ease with which Confederate troops overtook Arizona Territory in the summer of 1861, Union outposts in New Mexico were likely more than a little worried about the coming invasion. Flor is right here—this means the Union side would eagerly welcome stolen plans and documents from the Confederate army.

Page 31

Grace and Flor's plan here is far from outlandish—lots of women served as spies, on both sides of the Civil War! Women spies may even have had some advantages over men. Because of sexist stereotypes, men were more likely to view women as naive, innocent, or stupid— and therefore completely incapable of spying. Elizabeth Van Lew, a wealthy Virginia socialite, smuggled military secrets to the Union side (often hidden inside hollowed-out eggs) for the entire length of the war. Mary Bowser, a free Black woman, voluntarily posed as a servant in Jefferson Davis's Confederate White House so she could pass invaluable state secrets along to Union general Ulysses S. Grant. Pinkerton detectives including Kate Warne and Hattie Lawton helped foil an assassination attempt against Abraham Lincoln in 1861. Other famous Civil War women spies include Harriet Tubman, Rose O'Neal Greenhow, Pauline Cushman, Sarah Emma Edmonds, and many more.

Page 42

Although the population of Black people in New Mexico has never been large relative to other states, records show Black people living in this area at least as far back as the seventeenth century, during Spanish colonization. In 1860, the US census shows only a few dozen Black New Mexicans—but those numbers may be misleading. Many New Mexicans likely had a mixture of African, Latinx, Indigenous, or European ancestry by the time of the Civil War; and mixed-race people who could present and register as a non-Black person may have found advantages in doing so.

Page 43

High fashion of the nineteenth century tended to originate in Europe. Trends sometimes took as long as a year to make their way across the Atlantic to the United States—and then even longer to reach the landlocked western territories. Wealthy families on the Atlantic coast would've been the first to wear new English and French fashions. By hearing this insider report from Georgia via Grace, Luis can update his shop's selections and potentially edge out his competitors for a few months.

Page 45

Fun fact: Coat hangers weren't invented until 1869, so I had to come up with a different solution for how Luis would display sample dresses for his customers. Unless a tailor could afford tons of mannequins, wall pegs were probably the way to go.

Page 50

The bird-shaped object on the table is a sewing bird! This metal clamp could be attached to the side of a table, sometimes with a pin cushion on top of it. The bird's beak could open and then "bite" down on a piece of cloth, holding the cloth in place while a person worked on it.

Page 60

The building where the Confederate cotillion takes place is based on the Santa Fe Governor's Mansion, which wasn't built until 1870. I couldn't find any other historic buildings in the area in 1861 that had quite the look I was going for, so I ended up using it anyway! Mea culpa.

Page 66

A bunch of Confederates throwing a big party in the middle of what is technically Union territory is definitely bold but not totally out of the question. Plenty of Confederates and Confederate sympathizers populated New Mexico Territory, so a bunch of rich people having a party "just for friends" (and quietly discussing business in a locked back room) was—while risky—not impossible.

Page 76

The Confederates were really banking on Californian gold to help sustain them through the war, which is one of the reasons they were so eager to take over the western territories and start building rail lines. This, luckily, never quite *panned out* for them.

Page 97

The structure in the background is Fort Union, one of the main Union army strongholds along the Santa Fe Trail. This fort had to be rebuilt several times during the nineteenth century. The version Flor and Grace would have seen in 1861 was a short-lived earthworks structure—a giant mud fort! This fort helped defeat the Confederate invasion of New Mexico in 1862 but was in such a state of disrepair afterward that Union forces soon abandoned it. After the Union victory, a new fort was built in the same area, out of sturdier materials such as brick, stone, and lumber. It lasted until 1891. You can still visit the ruins of that final Fort Union today.

Acknowledgments

I'm indebted to a number of people for their help and support with this book. Thank you to Mey Rude and Sarah W. Searle for their invaluable feedback on early drafts of this story. To Dylan Edwards, for the thankless work he did helping to prepare each page for print, and for patiently listening to me babble about this book so many times. To all the incredible other writing and artist fellows of the Tulsa Artist Fellowship, whose friendship kept me grounded during so many late nights in the studio. To my secret Twitter friends, who I love. To all my Patreon supporters, who made it possible for me to turn down other work to focus on this book. To my amazing agent, Jen Linnan, who has been a tireless advocate for my work. To Greg Hunter, my editor, whose patience and good sense helped make this the best version of this book it could be. And to my family, for supporting me and believing in me even when my dream of making queer comics seemed like a far-fetched one.

About the Author

Melanie Gillman is an award-winning cartoonist and colored pencil artist who draws positive queer and trans comics for young readers. Their webcomic and graphic novel *As the Crow Flies* (Iron Circus Comics) has been named a 2018 Stonewall Honor Book, won the 2018 Excellence in Graphic Literature Award for Best Middle Grade Graphic Novel, and received nominations for an Eisner, Ignatz, and Dwayne McDuffie Award. In addition to their comics work, they are also an adjunct professor in the Comics MFA Program at the California College of the Arts.

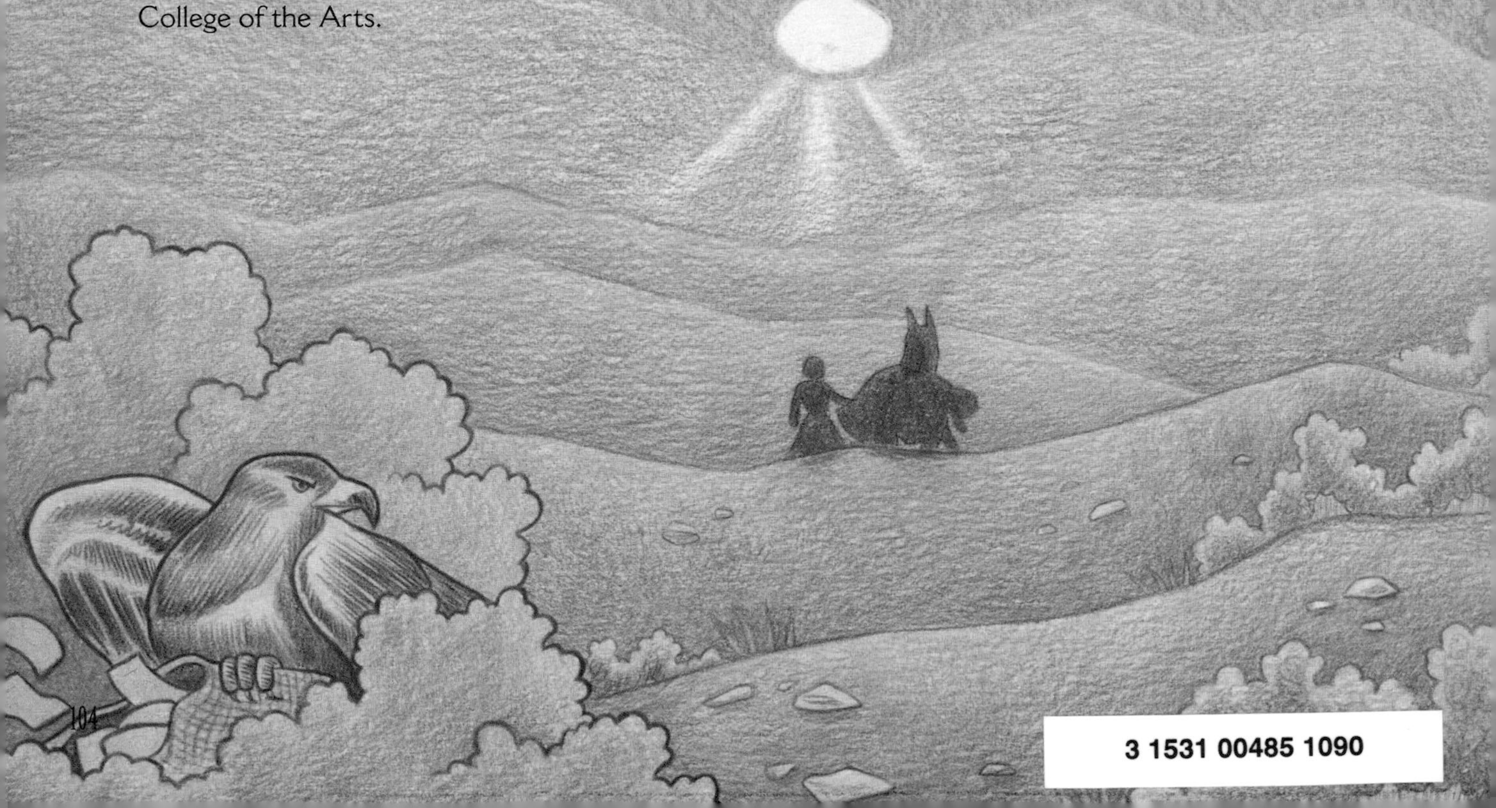